THE CHAMELEON CANDIDATE

THE CHAMELEON CANDIDATE

PAUL HARVEY JACKSON

JANUS PUBLISHING COMPANY
London, England

First published in Great Britain 2001
by Janus Publishing Company Ltd,
76 Great Titchfield Street,
London W1P 7AF

www.januspublishing.co.uk

Copyright © 2001 by Paul Harvey Jackson
The author has asserted his moral rights

**British Library Cataloguing-in-Publication Data.
A catalogue record for this book
is available from the British Library.**

ISBN 1 85756 535 5

Typeset in 10.5pt Baskerville
By Chris Cowlin, Janus Publishing

Cover Design Hamish Cooper

Printed and bound in Great Britain

*This book is dedicated to Alfreda
the perfect wife*

Chapter One

The sleek, black Chevrolet must have been busting a gut. Patrolman Toni Rossi, of the Mississippi State Police, came upon it suddenly as he rounded a bend on his motorcycle. The vehicle had ploughed into the parapet of a bridge. It now lay at a crazy drunken angle, protruding onto the highway. The high-pitched hiss of steam still gushing from the fractured radiator indicated the accident was recent.

Zebra stripes of light were already lazering the sky from the east as Rossi glanced at his watch; it said 05:00 hours. The highway illumination reflected thick, black tire marks where the driver had braked in a final desperate attempt at control.

Rossi cursed silently as he brought his machine to a juddering halt. He propped it on its stand on the hard shoulder. This was his last half hour of duty. He could have done without this. Accidents always spelt work, and by the look of this one it was truly 'molto sfavorevole'.

He approached the car with a sinking feeling, observing the New York license plate. There were bound to be casualties, almost certainly fatalities. The force of the crash had concertinaed the vehicle, ripping open the hood, so now it yawned wide like the jaws of some giant doomed crocodile.

The driver's door had been flung across to the other side of the highway, thus allowing a view of the carnage within. The sight that presented itself made even the battle-hardened cop catch his breath. The driver was dead. One glance was sufficient; his jugular vein had been severed by a chunk of windshield. Now his glazed eyes stared unseeingly at the sunroof.

Likewise, the man in the passenger seat was lifeless. The angle of his head indicated a broken neck. A further glance told Rossi he was an FBI agent. He could smell them a mile off. The man's badge inside his coat confirmed it.

But it was the passenger in the rear who really focused Rossi's attention. His tall bulk was sprawled across the seat. Immediately his dress set him apart as someone of consequence: silk tie, white silk shirt, Italian gray suit. Rossi could always spot the Italian cut.

Carefully he raised the head for a better look. The face had been badly cut by windshield glass and pieces of dashboard that had disintegrated. Despite the blood, something about the face jarred a memory cell within the cop. He felt for a pulse, eventually locating a tiny flutter.

Instinct told Rossi he was onto something big. This was no ordinary accident. An unusual feeling of inadequacy engulfed him as he withdrew from the vehicle and hurried back to his machine to radio for help.

He called the emergency ambulance service. Then he called his headquarters in Jackson. Sergeant Jed Cooper answered his call. In control now, Rossi conveyed the salient facts, adding that the face of the rear passenger appeared to be familiar.

'Wait out,' yawned the tired Cooper. It had been one of those nights. This was the third accident report. He was all done in.

Astride his motorcycle, Rossi watched the rapidly lightening sky. He had just taken the sixth drag from his Lucky Strike, when Cooper's Southern drawl crackled over the air.

'Jeez, Tony, yah sure kin pick the big 'uns!'

'Whaddya mean?' the irate Rossi snapped back. His longing for cool, white sheets was becoming an obsession.

'It's Nathan Beauregarde.'

'Who?'

'Beauregarde, Senator Nathan Beauregarde, the Third Party Presidential Candidate, yah lunkhead!'

The line went dead.

So that was why there was an FBI agent aboard, Rossi thought.

One

In the short space of time before the ambulance arrived, a shutter opened in his brain. The whole business fell into place. He managed the necessary flashback, to a bright afternoon in the fall in Manhattan several years previously, when he and his late wife Bella had been on a visit to New York. Bella had never been to the Big Apple before. They'd been so happy that day, window-shopping in Manhattan's turbulent Lower East Side. They were on their way to meet Bella's sister Touria and her husband Bruno.

Then it happened in a flash.

Out of an alleyway appeared two hoodlums. Within seconds, the couple was mugged. Bella's handbag was stolen. Worse, she was left unconscious on the sidewalk with severe head injuries.

Nathan Beauregarde had witnessed the assault from his office window across the street. He rushed to their aid. His timely assistance had almost certainly helped to save Bella's life, though she was destined to die of cancer the following year.

Now it was Rossi's turn to assist, to do what he could to repay that debt. His eyes welled up with tears as tender thoughts of his darling Bella swirled around his head.

Idle Winds, Mississippi, downstream some few miles from Natchez, is a small town, even by European standards. To even the most optimistic observer it has little to commend it. Like Topsy, it had obviously just 'growed'. Over the years it had nudged its way shapelessly out of the woods, lying lifelessly and unloved by the banks of the great Mississippi River.

Judging by the general expression of resignation on the faces of the inhabitants, even they were none too keen on this lost place. It was all too obvious that they were trapped, being too lily-livered to get out.

Situated as it was on one of the interminable bends of the huge, gray-green, mud-swollen Father of Waters, the whole place generated an ethos of what might best be described as silent, strangled suffering.

From late fall to early spring, a permanent river fog seemed to enshroud the place. It was in this place, in April 1945, that identical twin boys were born.

Selina Beauregarde, their mother, was a beautiful and strong-willed woman who owed something of her looks and stamina to her Cherokee grandmother. Despite this inherited stamina, she came within an ace of dying during that long and terrible night.

Winter had clung on much longer than expected to the river that year. A storm had got up late in the afternoon, persisting well into the night. The tar shack, where the heavily pregnant Selina lay, was attacked by a fierce storm, blowing in from the direction of the river. This increased in intensity as darkness fell.

Selina was attended by a Catholic midwife named Attracta O'Ryan, who seldom let her rosary beads stray far from her hands.

As was his custom in times of crisis, Thaddeus Beauregarde, Selina's husband, was nowhere to be found. Earlier in the day, at the onset of the seriously painful labor, she had dispatched him to bring back O'Ryan and the doctor. In the course of time the former arrived, but there was no sign of either Jethro Farley, the incompetent, drink-sodden, ex-Army surgeon, or Thaddeus. During some of her more lucid moments, Selina suspected, correctly as it turned out, that they had gone off together on some misplaced pre-emptive celebration.

The midwife was the illegitimate daughter of an Irish priest, Declan O'Ryan, who at one time had a parish down Baton Rouge way. She was a well-meaning, if somewhat inadequate, woman. In appearance she resembled, not surprisingly, a nun. Possessing no formal medical training, she had lived in Idle Winds since the dawn of time. Now in her seventies, she had over the years attended countless births, for the most part successfully. Everyone knew her, and respected her, albeit backwoods, skills.

Despite her great experience and strength of religious spirit, Attracta O'Ryan was frightened that night. She felt out of her depth. In between spasms of agonizing pain (Farley was supposed to bring the morphine), O'Ryan sat at the side of the bed helpless,

One

watching as Selina lay pale and for the most part silent, till the onset of further pain had her thin body writhing and twisting like an alligator being hauled tail first out of a swamp.

Watching and waiting and worrying about whether Selina's frail frame could take much more, Attracta O'Ryan must have said more Hail Marys that night than in a month of Sundays.

Dawn had just begun to make its presence felt in the sky as the midwife reached out to adjust the wick of the solitary kerosene lamp. Suddenly Selina shot up in bed, and in a clear steady voice cried out: 'Mano, dear God, Mano! They're yours. Why ain't yah here to help me?'

She fell back on the bed, her strength spent.

The very depth of emotion in her tone spooked the already overwrought midwife, and despite all her attempts to have Selina explain her remarks, not a word came from the prone form on the bed.

It was Mano she had said, not Thaddeus. O'Ryan was sure of that, the names were very different. She also knew that, despite her pain, Selina's mind was lucid. There was little doubt that the parentage of Selina's children was none of O'Ryan's business. She knew that the good time nightclub hostess was no saint, but by the same token she knew too that in the small, inward looking community of Idle Winds everyone liked to know everyone else's business.

It made her feel important that she was able to keep a finger on gossip. Then, when the time was ripe, she could filter it out, in exciting bite-sized chunks, to help to assuage nosy appetites.

Less than an hour later, just as the storm had begun to abate, identical twin boys were born to Selina Beauregarde.

Chapter Two

The first eighteen months of the little boys' lives in the tar paper shack on the banks of the river were probably no more hazardous than those of any other poor white trash kids of the period. They had the additional handicap of living in Mississippi, where such youngsters were, if possible, poorer than those in the rest of the states of the 'Slower South'.

As Selina, in her pain and distress, had already cried out, their father was indeed Mano le Cruz. Their conception was the result of one night of passion with this young Mexican charmer. A mining engineer, he'd been passing through Idle Winds, hoping to hitch a lift to the Gulf in search of work. For Selina, he was, without doubt, the most exciting thing ever to have hit the place.

Predictably, they clicked. She the local nightclub hostess, glamorous and sexually frustrated, he the roving Romeo. They drank and danced in the shabby nightclub, then later made love in his room in the run-down Hotel Metropole.

He reminded her of Gary Cooper, tall, dark, lanky and utterly charming. She reminded him of Jennifer Jones, with her demanding nature and sultry, brooding good looks. But despite this immediate bonding and her desperate attempts to persuade him to stay, he told her it could be nothing more than a one night stand. Idle Winds had nothing to offer him.

He was right. Next day he was gone, out of her life forever.

For a while Selina took a real interest in her children. Without doubt there was a certain novelty in giving birth to identical twins. Her interest was sufficient to see them christened in the tiny wooden Baptist Church. They were given the good old Biblical names, Nathan and Julius. Nathan was the elder by fifteen minutes.

Two

But, true to form, it wasn't long before boredom and resentment set in.

In time the kids grew to recognize her attitude, and to resent it.

The truth was that Selina never really wanted kids. She was sufficiently intelligent and self-aware to recognize that she was not emotionally cut out to be a mother, and never could be.

Up to this point her life, such as it was, had been that of a small town, good-time girl. She lived for the day, always with an eye to the main chance. She had been born downstream from Idle Winds, and every day of her life, for as long as she could remember, she had dreamed of 'quittin' this ole hole'.

The boys grew bigger, soon developing into dark, attractive looking babes. Soon their personalities began to take shape. Rarely could there have been two youngsters so utterly alike externally, yet with such very different natures. So alike were they that even their mother was unable to tell them apart.

At best Thaddeus Beauregarde, Selina's husband, was an intermittent father. At worst he was a nasty, drunken and abusive man, given to beating up and terrorizing both Selina and the boys. He was supposed to be manager of the seedy Blue Flamingo nightclub, where Selina was hostess, but in practice he was rarely there.

Soon it was the twins' sixth birthday. Money was still dreadfully scarce, and proper jobs, especially for coloreds and poor whites in Mississippi, almost non-existent.

Folk were only now beginning to realize that involvement in the war had cost the American people dear, much more so than the government cared to admit. Attitudes had changed, had hardened. In many respects the population, especially in the south, was no better off than it had been at the end of the depression years.

Even the implementation of the Marshall Plan, in the spring of 1947, designed to shore up war-torn European countries, particularly Russia (6 billion dollars credit for post-war reconstruction) was becoming a burden on the only country left that could possibly undertake the role of flagship of the western world in terms of influence and affluence.

The boom years of the fifties, the Eisenhower Years, which were to provide a much-needed respite amid the storms of the twentieth century, had still to arrive. People were in a vacuum, subdued, apprehensive, not at all acting like the victors of a world war. The truth was, despite all the talk and gerrymandering, nothing had really changed.

Into the bargain, many had lost loved ones, in Europe or the Pacific Campaign, at Corrigador, Guadalcanal, or in the steamy heat of the Malayan jungle. They, in particular, expected things to be better. But there was little evidence of it.

Roosevelt's New Deal, which undoubtedly helped folk survive the depression years, had given way to Truman's Fair Deal administration. But it mattered not who was at the helm, there was little improvement to the lives of the average person, and certainly no improvement to the lives of the poor folk on the Mississippi Delta.

Older people, who had survived the bad years, were conscious that this particular monster, far from being exterminated, had merely changed shape.

This shape was the Cold War, continuing poverty and increased racial violence. In other words, within twenty years a third monster had been created, one that the government, on the face of it, was doing little to contain.

The folk who lived in Idle Winds, or at least those who lived in the riverbank area where the Beauregardes lived, were, for the most part, in a time warp. They were kindly enough, but an odd bunch.

Old Matilde ran the local store. She was part Louisiana French and part Cherokee Indian, and a distant relation of Selina. She had enormous bony hands, more like flippers, a long chisel nose and a gentle crooning voice, as if she was permanently about to break into a lullaby.

Two

When she first saw the twins she crooned, 'Oh my Selina, what beautiful babes! I didn't think Thaddeus had it in him, must be the moonshine that done it. Lawdy days!'

She held each infant in turn, making strange clucking noises, for all the world like some old broody hen checking her chicks.

Then there was Fats McCausland, an enormous man, as the nickname implied. He was the local handy man and worked out of a hardware store. His family had emigrated from the north Antrim coast of Ulster many years before. They had been smallholders from beautiful Whitepark Bay, which enjoyed panoramic views over the Sound to Scotland, where on a clear day vehicles could be seen moving about on the Mull of Kintyre.

Even though Fats himself had never set foot on Ulster soil, somehow he managed to speak with a strong trace of County Antrim accent. Despite his huge, plain moon face, and a strawberry nose – the result of poor circulation, so he said – he fancied himself as a womanizer.

Fats had an equally plain wife, Martha. Martha was the Sunday School Superintendent. During the week her husband dominated her, but Sundays were different. Martha truly believed that Sundays formed the reason for which she had been brought into the world. Sundays were the days when she felt she had a purpose for living. Sundays were the days when she donned her best black dress, with thick Louisiana lace collar, black stockings encased in purple, button-back boots. Her attire was topped off with her Sunday hat, a truly magnificent affair, all set about with passion fruit, leaves and a dozen dangling cherries.

All the while she lectured her charges on the dangers of offending The Lord, the cherries would swing wildly about in gay abandon.

The minister of the tiny Baptist Church was the Reverend Sam McColgan. Of Scottish descent, his father had committed suicide in 1930 at the beginning of the Depression, when his business went bust. His mother died shortly afterwards, effectively leaving Samuel an orphan.

A clever young man, McColgan applied himself, made Bible College through winning a scholarship, and eventually became a minister. He'd been posted to Idle Winds as soon as he'd qualified in theology, and had never sought another parish, knowing that so much still remained to be done. McColgan knew how lucky he was to have such a thriving Sunday school in the hands of the devoted Martha McCausland.

The Beauregarde family's only real source of income was what Selina could earn as a hostess in the club. As her actual salary was non-existent, her cash flow consisted entirely of what tips she could prize out of satisfied clients. Her job was to entertain, to move in on customers and ensure their glass was always full, to sing, dance and generally make herself pleasant.

Thaddeus, her husband, had at one time been a partner in the club, but years of dissolute living had forced him to sell his interest. In theory he was now the manager, but the reality was that he was seldom there.

He had married Selina when she was eighteen and he was forty. In his own words, '...ah picked yah outa the gutter...' He created the job as hostess for her.

For a time she felt obligated to him, but soon he was using and abusing her. Within a few short years what respect and gratitude she'd had for him turned to fear and hate. For a long time now they had done little more than tolerate each other, both living their separate lives.

From the very start Nathan was a courteous and responsive little boy, with a built-in natural politeness, showing a strong desire to learn. Julius, on the other hand, was totally opposite in nature. He was a youngster who appeared to be hell bent on making his mark as the local bully.

Already, at the age of six, he was showing off, teasing and tormenting the other kids in the neighborhood. He was a born loner,

Two

self-centered and incapable of being a team player.

From that early age, unhealthy sibling rivalry began to rear its ugly head. This culminated in a particularly nasty incident, one that even shocked Selina. One day Julius found a hornets' nest down by the river. He ran back to the shack calling to his brother to come out to see it. As Nathan looked into the undergrowth, Julius hit the nest with a stick, and then took to his heels. Nathan's stings were so bad that he was in bed for many days. When she found out what had happened, Selina laid into Julius with her fists.

Ironically, despite such nasty traits showing in Julius's character, Selina found that she had a bonding with him that she just didn't have with his brother. The shy Nathan, even as a little boy growing up, always felt strangely ill at ease with his mother. He was never able to maintain eye contact with her for any length of time

As time went by Selina began to resent this in her elder son. Despite Julius's sly and destructive ways, there was no doubt she felt more comfortable with him. Whilst despairing of some of his activities, she was becoming proud of his undoubted charm, which he could turn on when it suited.

She began to feel that the studious goody two-shoes Nathan was altogether too up-stage for her, and she hated him for making her feel inadequate. 'Why, yah ain't like a chile at all!' she would chide him at frequent intervals, in her frustration.

For a while, Thaddeus appeared to be genuinely unsure whether the twins were his or not. Deep down he probably suspected they were not, for sex with Selina had, at best, been intermittent. But he was anxious to cash in on what kudos he could, for they were most attractive looking kids, and he was by now a far from attractive man.

Never much of a home bird, he had taken to disappearing for weeks on end. He would head over the border to Arkansas or down river into Louisiana, going on drunken gambling sprees, only to return weeks later without a dime in his pocket.

On one occasion he did return with a red dress for Selina, which he'd got in New Orleans. It was old fashioned, and Selina hated it on sight, considering that it didn't show off her figure to the best advantage. There was no way she was she going to wear it in the nightclub, as he wanted her to. In his rage at being thwarted, Thaddeus threw the dress out, poured kerosene over it, burning it to ashes.

In retaliation, the next time he went out, Selina threw out what whisky she could find, substituting kerosene in the bottles.

Jezebel Blackstock was a colored widow who worked as housekeeper to the Reverend Sam McColgan and his wife, Judy. She had one child, a little boy named Bobby. Bobby had an angelic face and round innocent eyes, encircled with eyelashes any girl would have died for. Apart from the occasional mild mischief associated with any five year old, there was nothing in his character that was remotely unpleasant. He was always anxious to please, offering to run errands or do odd jobs.

For some unknown reason, Julius deeply resented little Bobby Blackstock just as much as he resented his brother Nathan. At every opportunity he tormented and teased him. Apart from Bobby's mother, no one objected or tried to stop him. It just wasn't done for whites in Mississippi to come to the defense of colored folk.

Chapter Three

Up until the early 1960s, before the Martin Luther King years, Mississippi was not a good place for poor folk to be living in. This applied particularly to rural areas, where it didn't much matter whether you were white or colored, for the average standard of living was a couple of degrees above zilch.

Despite government initiatives, ostensibly designed to improve the lot of the coloreds, and just beginning to bite, an ominous undercurrent of racial violence had a nasty habit of pervading everything.

The reality was that poor whites were just as poor as their colored neighbors. All of them lived out their own private tapestry of anguish and dreams, desperately hoping to better themselves one day, but never really knowing just how to set about it.

The Ku Klux Klan, with its vicious courts martial, and blood curdling summary justice, was still very active in Mississippi and Alabama. Sinister segregation was very much the name of the game. The specter of it in schools, public transport and public amenities, in every area of life, was real and painful.

The fact that it was legal was bad enough, but that Southern whites considered it morally right, a hangover from the earlier belief that slavery was justified, was a particularly bitter pill for colored folk to be forced to swallow.

It didn't even just stop at segregation. Bullying, both physical and mental, together with beatings, were commonplace, with the occasional murder thrown in for good measure.

Into the bargain, it was of significance that not a single colored person from Mississippi had held elective office since the collapse of Reconstruction, almost a hundred years before. All sorts of unsavory intimidation was being routinely practised in order to keep things that way.

Nathan was a sensitive and observant boy. Growing up in this environment, he somehow felt that he was cut out for better things, for a better way of life, not only for himself and his family, but for his colored neighbors too.

From an early age he carried around with him a quiet feeling of purpose. This included a powerfully mature sense of injustice.

For a number of economic and social reasons, difficult to quantify, the State of Mississippi was particularly slow to pull out from post-war depression. For those who lived there, and it was heavily populated in certain areas, it seemed that the government in Washington was more than eager to help other countries, but not them.

As he grew older and his mind and senses matured, Nathan began to have the distinct feeling that Selina and Julius were ganging up on him, isolating him. At about the same time he came to the realization that Thaddeus was not his father. On the rare occasions that he saw him, any sort of paternal affection was completely lacking.

The little colored school that catered for the black children of Idle Winds, schools still being segregated, was little more than a ramshackle hut, situated at the end of a lane, close to the river. The sole teacher was a large, jolly colored lady, who went by the name of Miss Primrose. She had been pretty at one time and, according to those who remembered, slim. By this time she was well advanced in years, well past normal retiring age, and really beyond being able to deliver much meaningful teaching.

But she was kind and caring, gently mothering her twenty-eight young charges, hovering over them like some enormous dark chocolate hen. She could not deliver a particularly modern curriculum, she was not a font of academic knowledge. She could, however, deliver something that, in the long run, was infinitely more precious and useful to those underprivileged kids. That was

Three

an inner sense of security, a proper feeling of their own worth. This was a difficult and courageous thing to do in the racist climate of the time.

The actual school curriculum of this tiny school, or the primary school for white children further down river, had little to do with some of the out of school activities indulged in by the more adventurous pupils.

One of these was rattler bating, where a rattlesnake was pinned down by the head with a forked stick, while youngsters dashed around it in a circle, coming in closer and closer to its lethal, thrashing tail. Another was skinny-dipping, on moonlit nights in the deceptively slow and placid waters of that particular stretch of the river.

But the best one of all, a highly dangerous undertaking, one definitely banned by adults, was chicken swimming. Pocket money could be earned at this activity, which involved youngsters daring each other to swim the gauntlet of the huge froth-churning paddle wheels of the steamers as they chugged and threshed their way downstream to Baton Rouge or New Orleans. They had wheels the size of a house that forged up great swathes of water, glistening and sparkling in the sunshine like so many tiny incandescent shells.

Woe betide any crazy kid who swam too close, or misjudged, leaving it too late to clear the wheels; they would be dragged down by the undercurrent to be flattened against the steamer's stern like a hapless mosquito squashed beneath a Negro housekeeper's swat, or to be torn to pieces and strewn into the wheel itself, like so many shards of glass from a window shattered by a fast-moving baseball.

Selina had a friend, an Indian named Pretty Boy Beau Jangles. He was a distant relation, and his name was something of a misnomer, for he was neither pretty nor a boy. In fact he was just about the ugliest person that the boys had ever seen, with his scarred, wrinkled face and jet black hair that hung down to the small of his back, secured in a long pigtail by a strip of gater skin.

But he was exciting, patient and kind, telling the boys stories to make them laugh. He taught them backwoods skills, how to survive in the woods and how to fish for long, black conger eels with ten-foot willow rods. Eels with cold, mean, rheumy eyes, and teeth so sharp and jaws so strong that they could bite right through a man's hand to meet in the center. He showed them how to barbecue their catch, cutting the eels into kebabs, and smoking them over an open fire.

New Year's Day dawned bright and sharp. The clear, bitter light in the sky gave little clue as to what that day was to hold for poor, harmless little Bobby Blackstock.

For once there was little sign of river fog. It was a school holiday.

Bobby and some little colored pals were playing by the riverbank. Julius was roaming, looking for trouble, as usual. He linked up with Levi Hazzard, a youngster of his own age, another niggerhating youngster, whose father was a riverboat captain. The two rounded a bend and came upon the colored kids. Bobby, who'd been taken short, was pissing in the river.

'Let's put that notion outa him,' Julius said. 'We'll take a chance he's not. Too bad if he is, it'll hurt all the more!'

'Not what?' said Levi.

'Circumcised!'

As understanding dawned, a broad grin spread across Levi's face. 'OK buddy, y'er on!'

Julius searched in his pocket for a sharp instrument. He came up with a razor blade. 'This'll do. Right, move in!'

They pounced on the unsuspecting youngster, overpowering him and dragging him, screaming, into the undergrowth. The others took flight.

Young Bobby fought like a mountain cat. But it was useless. Hazzard pinned his arms behind him. Julius yanked down his pants and grabbed the little boy's tiny member.

'We're in luck! Yah'll not expose that in public again fer a while, yah lazy wee coon. This is white man's river!'

Three

'What yah goin ta do?' Bobby's eyes were rolling in his head with fear.

'Wait 'n' see!' With one quick slice, off came Bobby's foreskin. Blood trickled down his legs.

'Ah'll tell mah mamma. Ah'll tell everyfolk!' the little boy wailed, clutching his groin in agony. Shocked and deeply humiliated, with tears pouring down his face, Bobby cautiously pulled his pants up over the damage. Then, with a cry of frustration, he tore off into the undergrowth.

As for the bullies, they danced around in circles, whooping and yelling like a couple of dervishes.

Chapter Four

By the time little Bobby Blackstock had reached Reverend McColgan's house, where he lived with his mother, he had already decided to say nothing about his humiliating ordeal. He was a gutsy little fellow, and like most Mississippi coloreds, was becoming used to fighting his own battles.

In any case, he was a long way too embarrassed.

For a time, he had lingered in the woods till both pain and shame had become bearable. Then, when it became dusk, he began to be afraid. He decided to pluck up courage and make a run for home.

Before he entered the house, knowing that his mother would probably be in the kitchen, he dabbed a lump of cotton deep into the water butt at the back door. Holding this tight, he entered by the side door and tiptoed his way up the backstairs. He was in luck. He reached his own tiny attic bedroom without being seen, or, he hoped, heard.

He knew his mother would be worried about him, for by now it was dark. He also knew she liked him to report that he was back. For once he would have to forgo this.

He closed the door, sat on the bed, and cleaned himself up with the cotton. Then he took off his clothes and got into bed. He put the light off and awaited his mother's step on the stair. When she did put her head around the door, he pretended he was asleep.

Tomorrow was another day. He would have to think of some excuse to cover his unusual behavior. Lying in the darkness of the tiny room, he gritted his teeth. No one must ever know about his humiliation. Before sleep claimed him, he swore vengeance on his attackers. If either ever boasted about the

Four

attack openly, he would deny it.

Spring turned to summer and summer to fall with Thaddeus becoming worse. His behavior became more unreliable, his outbursts more frequent. Rarely was there a day when he was sober. It was only a matter of time before he lost his job at the nightclub. His one time friend and partner Hank Hopkins, who owned the club, could take no more. Thaddeus was driving away business. Hank opened the door of the club and physically threw him out. The following day Thaddeus left town and Selina was never to see him alive again.

In the week after Thanksgiving, Selina received a message from the sheriff's office in Natchez. A man's body had been found floating in the river. The description resembled that of Thaddeus. She was required to identify the body as that of her husband.

Old Silas Stack, who lost a leg fighting for the British against the Turks in Gallipoli in World War One, and had little to say to the world other than to mutter and spit and spit again, had been checking his rods for fish. He noticed what looked like a body, floating face down in the river. He hauled it in. He knew Thaddeus and thought it looked like him. He had then notified the authorities.

It was Thaddeus.

He was buried with the minimum of formality in Bethlehem Cemetery, beside a giant redwood tree. It was a cold and exposed place. A place where winter winds could blow cleansing draughts across his moldering bones.

He hadn't been a heap of good to Selina while he was alive, and certainly wasn't now that he was dead. His debts were not long in surfacing. As his widow, Selina became responsible for these. As it was, she had found it hard to make ends meet. Now she was desperate. Bailiffs honed in on her like bears to a honey pot.

Still slim and glamorous, she was not without offers of marriage, which came to her now that Thaddeus was dead. But the trouble was all the offers were from suitors who were almost as poor as she was. That was no good. Now, above all else, she needed financial security.

In the aftermath of Thaddeus's death, Selina began to develop an overwhelming desire to get away from it all. She wanted to quit Idle Winds forever; to go somewhere far, far away. To pull herself out of the swamp, to make a new start. To find somewhere, God knew where, a man, a worthy man, who would value and look after her. By all the law of averages, something had to happen to change her life for the better; she couldn't go on any longer feeling lower than a rattlesnake's belly. It did...

Pretty Boy Beau Jangles, whom she relied on even more now, agreed to take her to the Mardi Gras. The boys, almost eleven, were left to fend for themselves.

Selina found the key to her future in New Orleans. It came in the grotesque shape of Cyrus Bundy. Bundy, a wealthy rancher from Alabama, and a childless widower, was twenty-five years her senior. On the down side, he was just about the ugliest person she had ever met. They met in Crazy Joe's Bar on Bourbon Street.

Because the timing was right and she was utterly desperate, Selina set her cap at Bundy. Right away, she began weaving him into her web. Professional charmer that she was, it wasn't long before this lonely and unpleasant looking man fell under her spell. He was flattered by her attention, and she had little difficulty in drawing him further and deeper into the web, but as she was doing so some instinct told her to take her time about telling him of the twins.

Bundy was staying in the Grand Hotel at Lakeview, north of the city, while she and Beau Jangles were in a boarding house in Canal Street. As soon as Beau Jangles knew that Selina had baited her fish, he got out of the way. He would leave her to Bundy during the day, and only occasionally put in an appearance at night, linking up to enjoy the drink and some jazz.

Four

Bundy lavished money on Selina, wining and dining her, kitting her out from the best boutiques, and generally showing her off. He wanted her to move into the Grand Hotel with him, but, wisely, she decided to decline his offer.

By the sixth day of their courtship, not entirely unexpectedly, Bundy had succumbed to her charm, and proposed.

She accepted.

Only on the day she was due to return to Mississippi did Selina pluck up the courage to tell Bundy about her children. Unsure how he would react, she was anxious not to lose him. He had to know, for, self-centered as she was, she was not in the business of abandoning her boys. They needed a home too.

At first Bundy was both shocked and angry. He accused her of holding out on him. He had no experience of children, and told her forcibly that he had no wish to gain any. Finally, and very reluctantly, at the railway station, he agreed to a compromise. He would, as a special favor, take one, and only one, child. He would give the boy a home along with Selina as his wife.

Two kids were too much, especially identical ones. The very thought of them spooked him. It would mean far too much upset to his orderly household.

'Mah decision's made, honey. Take it or leave it!' Bundy glared defiance at her out of icy blue eyes.

She could see he was not for changing. His damp heavy purple lips, clamped around an enormous green Havana cigar, said as much.

'Jest the one gal, jest the one – yah choose. End of story!'

Shocked at this unexpected and unreasonable reaction, Selina begged and pleaded with him, saying that it was not fair to split them up. It would put her in an impossible position.

But she might as well have been talking to the wall in the station yard. He had switched off. Furthermore, she could see if she pushed the issue any further, she would be in severe danger of tipping the balance against her. She couldn't afford for that to happen.

The Chameleon Candidate

She'd had her say, and failed. Talking was at an end. For a long time she glared at him, trying to conceal the distaste she felt for him. She had not expected this reaction. 'What an ugly old boy you are,' she thought. 'Am I mad?'

But she knew well enough this was the best offer, financially, that she was ever likely to get. She'd been after money. She'd been offered it, plenty of it, she'd seen photographs of his beautiful ranch. With considerable self-knowledge, she knew she was sold on the thought of the money and power he was offering her. It was a done deal, and she knew it.

Bundy had no desire to go to Idle Winds with her. He had no wish to meet anyone from her old life, or the one offspring, a moment sooner than he'd agreed to. His marriage offer was genuine. It stood, but she must come to live with him in Montgomery and bring just one of her boys. But which one? Selina was left with that painful decision.

Little Bobby Blackstock soon recovered, physically at any rate, from his ordeal. But the mental scars, the dreadful humiliation at the hands of white boys, was another matter. The experience had changed Bobby from being a trusting little soul into a cautious youngster. He would never again be so trusting. He was a fair-minded kid, but he was determined to extract some kind of vengeance for what he'd suffered. The Reverend Sam McCausland would have been shocked if he knew just what dark thoughts his little Bobby was harboring.

Selina returned to Idle Winds with Beau Jangles to settle up her affairs. She was not without considerable lingering doubt about what she was being forced to do to Nathan. She had already made the decision during the journey home. It was Julius she was taking to Alabama.

What she needed now was time. Time to herself, time to work out plans for Nathan's future, before she said anything to anybody. Beau Jangles was the only one who knew, and she swore him to secrecy.

Four

Days went by, and still Selina had said nothing. She was beginning to discover that to find the right moment was even more difficult than she had imagined.

Then, one morning she was sorting through her things and thinking hard about the future, when she came upon a Christmas card in a bag. It was from her Aunt Nessie Connor in New York. The card said she was lonely and greatly missing her husband Vinnie, a New York policeman, who had died from a heart attack two years previously. They had no children.

Suddenly Selina had a brainwave. She would offer Nathan to Aunt Nessie! Nessie had never met either of the boys, but Selina had once sent her a photograph of them, and the older woman had appeared to be very taken with them. But would she actually take Nathan now? Would she give him a home? He was a clever little boy. God knew she was aware of that. He was well behaved and would be no trouble.

Next day she wrote to Nessie, putting forward her proposition. Wisely she decided to await the response before saying anything to the boys. After all, if Nessie declined, Selina would still be faced with a problem that could prove to be insoluble. She had to say in her letter why she was forced to split them up. Thaddeus had died, she had been offered marriage, but her prospective husband would only take one child.

She knew in her heart she was asking a very great deal of her aunt, but she felt that she had no choice. She would not, could not, allow Nathan to be put in care just to fuel her own selfish ambitions.

For the next few weeks Bobby Blackstock stayed well clear of both Julius and Levi Hazzard. He was biding his time. Then, one day in early April, with the trees beginning to take on their spring foliage, and the sun glistening off the water of the great Mississippi River, he got his opportunity.

From time to time Bobby would fish alongside Old Silas. Over the years the old man, who enjoyed well-behaved young company, had given Bobby things that he'd carved from driftwood. One day he gave the youngster a knife. It was a real fisherman's knife, with all sorts of attachments. Best of all, it had a long sharp blade with a finely honed point. The knife was the pride and joy of Bobby's life. It went everywhere with him, even under his pillow at night. School over, Bobby wandered alone by the river bank, watching the passing traffic chugging up and down, wondering where it was all going to.

Suddenly, he heard a scream. He ran in the direction of the cry. He rounded a bend and saw Julius and Hazzard bating a little colored boy, Mattie Jackson, who was one of his classmates.

'Run Mattie, go!' he shouted, engaging the attention of the bullies.

Mattie didn't need to be told twice. He shot into the undergrowth. Moments later, with total disregard for his own safety, Bobby hurled himself at the two. Momentarily they were taken aback by the ferocity of the assault. But they were bigger, and there were two of them. They closed with him. Julius yanked off his trouser belt ready for use. Bobby, trusty knife in hand, moved in for the attack. The sun glinted off the blade.

'Watch out, he's got a knife!' Hazzard shouted.

Julius threshed out wildly, using the belt as a lasso, attempting to flick the knife from Bobby's hand. On came the colored boy, heading straight for Julius. His blood was up. He wanted revenge.

Julius sidestepped him, but Bobby would not be deflected. He turned and made another charge at Julius.

Windy now and, like all bullies, easily scared, Julius shouted to Levi, 'Get behind him, jump him from behind!'

Obediently, Hazzard sprang onto Bobby's shoulders, knocking him forward. This action forced the knife into Julius's stomach. With a gurgling noise in his throat, Julius dropped to the ground, clutching his stomach. Blood was dripping through his fingers.

Four

'Yah've killed me, yah've done fer me, yah little black bastard!' He lay writhing on the ground.

Seized with panic at what he'd actually done, Bobby cut and ran. He didn't dare to look behind. He ran without stopping for well over a mile, still clutching the bloodstained knife. He headed for the woods. Now in fearful mental turmoil, he stayed crouched at the base of a huge redwood tree till it was dark, terrified to go home or to meet anybody, for they would know something terrible had happened.

He had no idea if he'd actually killed Julius. He prayed that he hadn't. It was little comfort that he hadn't meant to wound him, just to stick him perhaps, draw a little blood, give him a fright. But when Hazzard had landed on his back, he was forced forward.

He made it to his bedroom with his luck holding. Once again his mother would wonder where he was, but he didn't see her, and she'd left the back door open. He dreaded what the morning would bring. But, come what may, he had got his revenge!

Next day, greatly to his relief, no one passed any remarks that could have referred to the incident. This told him it had not been sufficiently serious to be a talking point. As it turned out, Julius's wound, despite the amount of blood, turned out to be relatively minor. It needed some stitches, but, for obvious reasons, Julius was not anxious to draw attention to it. Instead, he bathed it in cold water, holding cotton against it, till the bleeding stopped. Despite the lack of serious damage, and because it was not stitched, there would always be a scar...a scar he would have to try to conceal from Selina.

Selina's luck was in. Within a fortnight, Aunt Nessie had written back to say she would take the boy. Nathan would stay with her in her small Manhattan apartment until he was of an age to fend for himself. She accepted that he would be company in her old age. The letter ended with good wishes to Julius and her in their new life in Alabama.

The boys took the news that they were to split up better than Selina had dared to hope. The truth was they had never been friends, never developing any brotherly feeling for each other. Even though neither had seen their new homes, nor the folk who were offering them, both appeared to view the moves as something of an exciting challenge. They were old enough to recognize that Idle Winds, Mississippi, had little to offer them or their mother.

The news was broken to them on their twelfth birthday. By the end of the week they were to be split up. Selina had telephoned Aunt Nessie telling her she was putting Nathan on the night train to New York. Then came the parting of the ways. Beau Jangles accompanied them to the railway station. Nathan boarded the train heading north. Selina and Julius, the train for Alabama.

Their new lives had begun...

Chapter Five

Next morning, Aunt Nessie met Nathan at New York Central Station. They experienced an immediate bonding. Aunt Nessie was small, bustling, kindly, with her gray hair scooped back in a bun. She reminded Nathan of a cartoon granny. She had a warm smile that lit up her whole face, a smile that said everything to this lonely boy.

'My, but you're a good looking boy! I'm real surprised your momma could bear to part with you. What a lovely way you speak!' she gushed.

Nathan blushed, not knowing where to look. This tiny woman, in her seventies, who had always longed for children of her own, had a prominent motherly instinct in her.

They took a taxi from the station to her apartment. It was about fifteen minutes drive from the station. It was in a modern apartment block, off Whitehall Street, overlooking Battery Park, in Lower Manhattan. During the drive, Nathan was fascinated by the sheer volume of traffic, the buzz and power coming from the roads and sidewalks. He had never seen anything remotely like this in his life. He'd never seen even one skyscraper; now the skyline was littered with them.

Aunt Nessie, her voice filling with pride, pointed out the main ones: the Empire State Building, the Chrysler Building, Trump Tower, and the Flatiron. She was glad to be able to give him a quick résumé of her city. She had never lived anywhere else in the whole of her life, nor had she wanted to. To her, there was nowhere else that could possibly compare with the Big Apple.

Traffic in front, traffic beside, traffic behind them, all constantly throughout the short journey. At times, Nathan was convinced traffic was on top of them as well; all noisy, honking horns, revving engines, thrusting, pushing, downright anxious to get to their destinations, impatient of those who got in their way. He felt exhilarated and a little nervous, as Aunt Nessie chatted incessantly in the rear of the large yellow taxicab.

Aunt Nessie's apartment was on the twelfth floor of a twenty-floor block. Nathan was mightily impressed with the view; the Brooklyn and Manhattan bridges spanning the Hudson to one side, the Statue of Liberty and Ellis Island, in the far distance, to the other.

His fascination was ongoing. He had never been in an elevator before. Then, to his delight, he discovered that he had his own small room, with his own furniture. In the tar shack in Mississippi there were only two bedrooms, he'd been forced to share one with Julius. This was luxury indeed.

Within a week or two Nathan began to feel at home in this vast, noisy metropolis. Already, memories of his deprived Southern existence were beginning, if not to fade, at least to get a little blurred at the edges.

Aunt Nessie had already shown him some of the sights of the city, in particular Central Park. He became fascinated at the thought that such a huge park offering so much – lakes, gardens, fountains, even a Museum of Art – could be situated right in the center of the busiest city in the world. This was the beginning of a love affair with Central Park that was to last for the rest of his life. In times of crisis, or merely for mental relaxation, he would always head for his beloved park.

Aunt Nessie enrolled him in his new primary school, a large school, with over a thousand pupils, off Union Street in Brooklyn. The school, run by the Catholic Church, had an excellent teaching record, enjoying a large catchment area for pupils from every walk of life. The headmaster, Dominic Downie, was a huge man with a flowing beard. He was a well-known and respected academic. A disciplinarian, he stood no nonsense, but had the gift of extracting the best from his pupils.

Five

Each morning Nathan would cross over the Brooklyn Bridge by bus, returning late in the afternoon. Mentally mature for his age, he had, to the delight of his teachers, a way of approaching study that was both responsible and enthusiastic. It wasn't long before he integrated himself with staff and classmates alike. Apart from the occasional dig at his Southern drawl, all were happy to accept him. Soon Aunt Nessie, now his official guardian, was receiving glowing reports from his teachers.

Selina and Julius also reached their destination; Montgomery, Alabama, which was to be their home from now on.

Selina knew that the whole business was probably foolhardy and certainly fraught with risk. For a start, she knew almost nothing about the man she was to marry, apart from the little that had suited him to let slip at the Mardi Gras. She'd had no contact with him from the day she left New Orleans, apart from a single phone call she had made to advise him of the date and time of arrival of her train. She had no way of knowing if he would be at the station to meet them. Now that she had time to think, she was beginning to realize just what a horrifying amount she had taken at face value.

Perhaps he wouldn't be there at all? Perhaps he was a fraud, just some ugly old boy shooting off his ugly mouth when he'd lowered enough booze, flattered that he'd got the attention of a glamorous woman. Perhaps he didn't live in that grand ole ranch at all. Perhaps the photographs that he had shown her had been of someone else's ranch. Did he have a criminal past? Perhaps she had dreamt the whole damn thing out of sheer desperation and wishful thinking. Then she recalled that he had given her his telephone number, and when she rang, he had answered it. She would just have to wait and see.

What she did know for sure, and this had not changed, was that she had a pathological desire to get away from Idle Winds, to start a new life. She was sick, oh so very sick, of being dirt poor. She was sick of scraping along a yard above the gutter. She had only one life, nearly half of it already gone. If a little risk taking was needed in order to improve her lot, and Julius's, then so be it.

All these uncomfortable and negative thoughts flashed through her mind as the train rumbled its slow way to Montgomery. Selina glanced over at Julius seated opposite her in the carriage. In the whole of her life she had only really loved one person, one person who had fired up all her love and lust for life, and that was only for a fleeting moment. That was all that fate had allowed her.

It certainly wasn't Thaddeus, whom she'd married when she was too young and on the rebound. He had convinced her that she could go for the big time in her career as a nightclub hostess. Far from giving her the bright lights and fame she craved for, he'd caused her more heartache than she cared to remember.

Nor was it Cyrus Bundy, the wealthy, but far from charming, elderly rancher, with whom she'd agreed, on some crazy impulse, to marry and spend the rest of her life.

No, it was Mano le Cruz, the young Mexican charmer, the father of her children, who had stolen her heart and run off to the Mexican Gulf with it.

Without him noticing it, Selina studied Julius's face. She wasn't exactly bowled over by the expression it held, but the pure physical beauty of it was something that made her heart beat fast, so fast that she thought it might thump right out of her chest. Surely no one could be considered a failure who was capable of producing such a beautiful child?

Julius turned and caught her studying him. Embarrassed, she moved her head to look out of the window.

She said, 'Jesus, don't this train move slow?'

He didn't answer. She was glad.

When Thaddeus was alive he clung to the illusion that the children might be his. She'd let him think it, it made her life that much easier. In any case she had little energy to spare on fruitless arguments about that subject. It was sufficient that she knew the truth.

Five

In the event, Cyrus Bundy was as good as his word. He was at the station, awaiting their arrival. Showing no sign of affection, he directed them out to a huge white Pontiac waiting in the station yard. On the hood was a logo of a silver bull. In the cold light of day, Bundy seemed to be even more ugly than she remembered when she first met him in the half-light of Joe's Bar on Bourbon Street.

Walking to the car, she was struck by an acute attack of nerves. She looked anxiously at Julius for his reaction, but to her relief he seemed to be more taken with the Pontiac than the ugliness of Bundy. She breathed a sigh of relief. Perhaps she was overreacting. She only knew that she felt very vulnerable at that moment. If Julius had shown any antagonism towards Bundy, she would have headed straight back to Mississippi.

The journey to the ranch, about twenty minutes drive at a fast pace, was conducted in virtual silence. Selina let Julius sit in the front seat. She was more comfortable viewing Bundy from behind. He wore a ten-gallon hat, and his neck was so fat and pockmarked that even from that angle he was repulsive.

Bundy lit a cigar, and soon the inside of the car was wreathed in fumes. Selina was glad. It provided her with a smokescreen for her to be alone with her thoughts. Uppermost in her mind was the thought of having to succumb to such a creature in the marriage bed. When she saw her new home, however, all that was forgotten, at least for the present. The ranch was magnificent.

With a few reservations, Nathan began to enjoy his new life in New York. Quiet and likeable, shy and superficially friendly, he was not a boy to make enemies. Soon he found himself thinking less and less about Mississippi days. He'd promised to send Beau Jangles a postcard of the Statue of Liberty. He did this, but got no reply. He played sports like any other twelve year old, mainly baseball and football, but with no great enthusiasm. He was not a natural ball player, lacking the necessary aggression that won games. Nor, unlike his brother, was he really street-wise. His basic nature was too gentle to allow for that.

On his thirteenth birthday, Aunt Nessie threw a small party for him and a few of his school friends. By now she was oozing with pride and wanted to show him off to the other parents.

At about that time Nathan was to discover an interest in politics deep within him. The seed had been sown by a gifted teacher. A chord had been struck in the boy, one that was destined to grow louder and louder.

The teacher, Norbert O'Farrell, an Irishman who lived in Greenwich Village, taught history and politics to the senior boys. He had the Irishman's gift of the gab, and held a fascination for Nathan, who lapped up everything that he said.

During the whole of the year that Nathan had been in New York, he had not heard anything from his mother. Consequently, he had no idea if she and Julius had reached Alabama, or if she had married the man named Bundy.

After some days of indecision, he decided it was time to write to his old friend, the Reverend Sam McColgan, requesting news of his family. He received a courteous letter back, full of apology that there was no news for him. No one in Idle Winds had heard anything. The letter ended with the fervent hope that Nathan was going to church on a regular basis.

In actual fact, he was. Aunt Nessie, a devout Roman Catholic, had encouraged him to come with her each Sunday to Grace Church in Gramercy, a ten-minute bus ride away. This was not the religion to which he'd been accustomed, and was very unlike the simple Southern Baptist faith of his childhood. He knew he could never get into the confession mode demanded by his Aunt's church. But for the present, he accompanied the old lady. He wasn't sure whether the Reverend McColgan would have approved!

Some of Selina's lingering doubts about the folly of her decision to

Five

marry Bundy were dispelled the next day, as surely as the morning mist is dispersed by the heat of the sun, when she saw the ranch properly in daylight. It had been dusk the previous night by the time they arrived at the ranch, which hadn't allowed a proper view of her new home.

Set in a thousand acres of prime grazing land some thirty miles south west of Montgomery, the ranch must surely have been the dream of every ambitious Southern Belle. It was not old. Bundy had had it built for his first wife, in the old cotton plantation style, some twenty-five years previously. Pure white, the front of the house was complemented by a graceful verandah. Stately pillars stood four square on each side of the magnificent entrance porch.

Inside, the house had eight bedrooms and four reception rooms. The hall was a masterpiece of Southern architecture, the focal point being a priceless cut glass chandelier. Out of the hall floated a gently curving staircase leading to the upper floor. At the rear was a centrally heated, indoor swimming pool. To Selina's surprise, the four house staff were all colored. So, she was to be the mistress of all this! It was all worthwhile then, the leap in the dark, and the uncertainty...

Bundy showed them over the house in his usual snappy manner that she was beginning to get used to. To his delight, Julius was allocated a small bedroom to the front of the house. Selina and Bundy's bedroom – he was not waiting till after their marriage, to share – the master bedroom, was luxurious. It had an en-suite bathroom, with gold fittings. She had to pinch herself at regular intervals to ensure she wasn't dreaming.

That night they dined well, waited on hand and foot. Selina drank too much, excited and overwrought by her newfound status. If she drank too much, Bundy drank twice as much. If his complexion had not already given the clue about his drinking, all she had to do was flashback to Mardi Gras, and the amount he lowered during that time. Now here he was, knocking it back again, like there was no tomorrow, on his own stomping ground. Despite her artificially created internal warmth, a small cold frog jumped in her heart. Once again, she was getting involved with a hardened drinker.

Over the years, thanks mainly to Thaddeus, she had become something of an expert on the effects of drink on men. With some, the minority, it made them open, lively and amusing. As for the others, it made them morose, bitter, prone to self-pity, often to violence and abuse. It seemed, as she watched Bundy's reactions sprawled over the huge dinner table, that he fell into the latter category.

She did find one aspect of the master bedroom that pleased her; it contained two single beds, albeit large ones. She recalled requesting this on the night Bundy proposed to her. He had said little about it at the time, so she had no way of knowing if he would keep his word. In the event, Bundy was either too tired or too drunk to demand his conjugal rights.

Next day, he drove them around some of the estate by jeep. They were shown over the stables, and spoke to the staff. Bundy owned three racehorses, looked after by his personal trainer, a tiny man who was an ex-jockey by the name of Milt Tolliver. Bundy took great pride in telling them that all three had won races all over the State. In particular, a jet-black mare called Arlene, after Bundy's first wife, had won the Alabama Derby. Despite certain mental adjustments she'd been obliged to make, Selina couldn't help feeling that she too had picked a winner. So what that Cyrus Bundy didn't look like Cary Grant, you couldn't have everything in life.

In New York, Nathan had become genuinely fond of Aunt Nessie, and grateful to her as well. At the same time, he was becoming aware that he was in danger of being smothered by her. For a while he enjoyed this new feeling of being spoiled, of being special to someone. But after a while it began to get on his nerves. The trouble was that he was a very private boy, and Aunt Nessie needed to be told everything. He was not used to this inquisitiveness, even

Five

though he knew it was done with the best possible motives. Back in Mississippi, Selina had not been in the spoiling business. If there was any spoiling to be done, it was usually directed at herself.

Now that she had this young man all to herself, Aunt Nessie was making up for lost time. She was becoming terribly possessive. Nathan found it hard to cope. He had to try to steer a middle course. On the one hand, he tried desperately not to offend her; on the other hand, he put out feeble signals that she might just be crowding him a little. In his anxiety not to hurt her, Nathan soon found himself getting close to telling her lies. He started embroidering the truth, telling her things he felt she wanted to hear. Despite these irritations, he knew that he could have fared a great deal worse. He could have been fostered by some old dragon who resented his very presence.

In Alabama, Bundy pressed ahead with the wedding arrangements. Even though she could hardly bear to look at him, Selina was still under the impression that she knew what she was doing. She was doing it for security for herself and Julius.

With regard to the bedroom, she was relieved to note that, on the face of it, Bundy did not appear to have much of a sex drive. Perhaps she could get away without doing it altogether?

When she first met Thaddeus, he'd been quite good-looking, wholesome at any rate. Even at the end, when he had become bloated and discheveled through drink, he was still a prince compared with Bundy, this huge, clumsy man, with his wet mouth and row of discolored teeth.

In all, Bundy employed twenty staff on his ranch. As far as Selina had been able to observe, he didn't do any work on the ranch himself. He told her he had an office in Montgomery, but not where it was, nor what he did there. She could see he didn't encourage her to pry into his personal affairs. Consequently, she had no idea as to the source of his income.

As those early days went by, Selina met all the ranch hands, including the foreman, Jock McIvor who was a tall, thin and very dour Scot. They were all respectful enough to this outsider, but remote too. She knew she could never make friends with any of them. She also knew that she would be unable to find out anything more about the man she was to marry from them.

Another matter puzzled her. Despite the fact that Montgomery, Alabama was every bit as bad as Mississippi for displaying racism of the worst kind, why were all Bundy's household staff colored? She'd already worked out that he was a racist. Perhaps he enjoyed employing them as servants, subordinates – even using them as latter day slaves? He certainly appeared to have little affection for them, speaking to them abominably at times.

But this enigma, and others that were beginning to surface in her mind, was of secondary importance. Her star was rising. A short while ago, she was a poor white trash nobody. Now she was the fiancée of one of the wealthiest and most powerful men in all Alabama. She began to take on a permanent up-beat attitude, as she savored all this in her mind.

The wedding was a surprisingly quiet affair, with only a few ranch staff present. Bundy had nobody on his side, no family to represent him. He had never talked about any family, only his first wife, with no details as to how she had died.

Selina looked radiant in an apricot colored outfit. Her clothes contrasted strikingly with the natural darkness of her skin. She was given away by Julius. The ceremony was very simple, performed by a local Baptist minister in the garden of the ranch.

That evening the couple flew off to Paris for the honeymoon. Bundy had booked a suite in the Ritz Hotel, in Place Vendome. This was within walking distance of the shops on Rue de Rivoli and Boulevard Haussman. Selina was utterly fascinated with the style and wealth. It was a totally different way of life from what she'd been used to, and it was Bundy who'd brought her here. He had been to Paris before, and was soon showing off his knowledge of the city. They dined in style in many restaurants, including dinner

Five

on a Seine bateau. The clothes-conscious Selina was thrilled by the beautiful boutiques. When Bundy could draw her away from these, they visited art galleries and museums, including the Louvre. The nightlife was another thrill. Each night they would go to a different show.

Despite the fact that she was in the city of her dreams with Bundy showering presents on her, Selina could not rid herself of a nasty feeling that he was not all he pretended to be. She couldn't really work out what it was that he was pretending to be in the first place. She began to detect a sinister undercurrent to the man. Predictably, he drank heavily during the two weeks they were in Paris. And it was during one of these drinking sprees that he let things slip, boasting in an unguarded manner about matters Selina would have preferred not to hear. This made her suspect that his wealth had been acquired by devious, even unlawful, means.

Soon she began to find it difficult to quantify her feelings towards him. Already disenchanted with his physical appearance, now she was beginning to find that his character was suspect. This time spent with him alone was quickly doing a good job of reversing the positive feelings she had begun to experience before they left Alabama. All these negative and alarming thoughts began to crowd in on her as her instincts, once again, were starting to tell her she might have made a dreadful mistake. What were his motives for marrying her at all? Had he married her for feminine company? It was obvious that he was not a man to be bothered with small talk. But small talk and companionship were all she had to offer. She had plenty of questions, but no answers. She couldn't forget that he'd proposed to her after a vast quantity of bourbon had been consumed. Admittedly, she had wanted him to propose, but more and more she was beginning to wonder, why had he? By the same token, he'd had plenty of time to sober up, to reflect. If he hadn't wanted to go through with it, all he had to do was not meet them at the station, or hang up on her when she telephoned.

It was all a great mystery, and not a very pleasant one. Perhaps, after all, she was not destined to get to grips with the happiness and security her spirit craved. Then again, all might be well when they got back to the Alabama sunshine. Her overwrought imagination had gone into free-fall in this city of love; a return to more familiar surroundings might ease her mind.

With the stable background Aunt Nessie had undoubtedly given him, Nathan's progress from Junior School to High School, was as steady as it was predictable. His new school, St Christopher's High School, off West 111th Street, was at the northwestern tip of Central Park.

In his fifteenth year, Nathan had become an avid reader, a serious seeker after knowledge. In particular, he read that all was not well in his native Mississippi. The Southern Civil Rights Movement had gotten under way, with some good work being done. Even better, in the previous year, the Interstate Commerce Commission had ordered the desegregation of bus and train stations. This was a major development, something that this earnest young man was delighted to hear about. Deep down he cared about the less fortunate folk he'd left behind.

For a young white man of his age and time, Nathan Beauregarde had a highly developed sense of Civil Rights. He had witnessed at first hand as a small boy growing up in rural Mississippi, just what a cruel and unjust society it still was for black people. Now, after school, instead of playing baseball in the parks, or knocking about the streets like most youngsters, he spent endless hours in public libraries, soaking up knowledge.

One afternoon he was browsing in the Manhattan Municipal Library, when in came a young man in his mid-twenties. Tall and good looking, he had a striking presence and Nathan thought he looked a little like President Kennedy. He made his way to the bookcase beside Nathan, and began working his way through some law books. There was something about him that made Nathan unable to take his eyes off him. This was just as well, for he was able

Five

to see a youth slide up behind him, put his hand in the man's back pocket, and extract his wallet.

'Hey, cut that out!' Nathan shouted, and made for the pickpocket, who was already heading for the door. He broke into a run but, moving fast, Nathan managed to head him off before he reached the street. The wallet flew out of his hand, as Nathan struggled with him. Realizing what had happened, the startled victim came over. He picked up his wallet, and then grabbed the pickpocket by the scruff of the neck.

'Will you accept my punishment, or will I call the cops?' the man asked calmly.

The thief looked at him blankly for a moment, then said, 'Yours Mister, yours!' He was not used to such options.

By now some of the customers and library staff had gathered around.

'I feel sure it is of little use to ask your name, you'll surely tell a lie.' The man spoke with a beautifully cultured voice. 'Let this be a lesson to you, young sir. Mark my words, I possess a photographic memory for faces. If ever I see yours again, you'll be in trouble, understand? Now get out of my sight!' The pickpocket gave a surly nod and the man let him go, but not before administering a powerful kick to his backside, which propelled him headlong into the street.

Mightily impressed, Nathan stood watching, his mouth hanging open. The man was grinning. 'Summary justice, it works every time. Saves so much hassle! I can't thank you enough, young sir. There are things in that wallet I would have had difficulty in replacing.'

He held out his hand. 'My name is Mayo Cleveland, what is yours?'

Nathan told him.

'Here, please do accept this.' Cleveland pushed a twenty-dollar note into his hand.

'No, I. . . I can't,' stammered Nathan, but Cleveland was insistent.

That evening Nathan told Aunt Nessie about the incident in the library, and how much he'd been impressed with the man called Mayo Cleveland.

'My, that's a coincidence,' the old lady said. 'I think I know about him. Brewster Cleveland was a lieutenant who served with your Uncle Vinny. He was gunned down over in Queens a while back. I met his mom only last month . . . aged something dreadful, poor woman. Told me she was living over Rivington way. Her son, Mayo, I'm sure she said, is a law lecturer at the University of New York. Now there's a coincidence for you!' She rocked back and forth in her chair at the thought of it. Nathan thought it an extraordinary coincidence as well.

On their return from honeymoon, Bundy enrolled Julius in an all-white school on the outskirts of Montgomery. Julius was not particularly pleased to see them home, in particular his stepfather, whom he was beginning to dislike. His two weeks of unfettered freedom around the ranch had come to an abrupt end.

Unlike his highly motivated twin up north, it soon became obvious that Julius had neither the desire nor capability to learn. As in Mississippi days, he considered school to be a total waste of time. His behavior was an extension of what it had always been. He was a rebel without a cause. The destructive traits that had formed in his character when he was younger were still there, only more deeply embedded. There was no doubt that for those with eyes to see, or care, Julius Beauregarde was already well down the road towards becoming a serious misfit. His dislike of blacks, already well distilled in his make-up, was only reinforced by what he saw around him in Alabama. His favorite saying, slipping off his tongue a dozen times a day was, 'The only good nigger's a dead one!' But Selina, something of a serious misfit herself, had no eyes to see the deterioration in the character of her son. She was struggling with her own growing doubts and troubles.

Daily, despite the vastly improved quality and style of her new life, she found herself battling against isolation and disappoint-

Five

ment. She had little desire to feel this way. It certainly had not been her intention. Superficially, many of her dreams had come true. But there was something not right in her relationship with Bundy, something that she had a horrible feeling could only get worse.

The truth, and now she could see it, was that she didn't, and never really could, belong to Bundy's world. She had become eternally ill at ease with his staff, who would only take orders from Bundy. She was the outsider, and they seemed determined to keep it that way. The one bright spark in her darkening gloom was that Bundy still had not sought to have her in bed. Instead, he contented himself by coming in at all hours of the morning, falling drunk into his bed and snoring the rest of the night away like the pig he was.

Several times, during those painfully lonely and revealing days after her return from honeymoon, Selina sat down fully intending to write to Nathan. Each time something held her back. Perhaps subconsciously she felt she had let him down, had abandoned him without a fight.

It had always been her intention to re-unite her sons one day. She had hoped to look on the 'Alabama Period' as one of financial and spiritual reconstruction, a time that would allow her to consolidate her position as a mother till she got her family together again. She had thought naively that Bundy would not live long. He was, after all, twenty-five years her senior. When he did die, she would have the money and power to be able to offer both of the boys something substantial.

But it was Bundy's attitude from the start, his insistence that she brought only one boy, which had split the family and made all her dreams turn sour. In the grip of her present frame of mind, it was impossible for her to contact her clever son. Perhaps next year, when the sun shone again. She wished with all her heart that she had never set eyes on Cyrus Bundy.

Chapter Six

Despite the many doubts assailing her, Selina made a valiant effort to make her new life work. It was, after all, the kind of lifestyle she had been promising herself for a very long time.

After the novelty of the honeymoon had faded, Bundy became a virtual mute. He spoke to her as little as he could get away with. Still, Selina had no idea how he spent his days when he wasn't about the ranch, where he went or whom he saw. In the absence of hard information, she supposed he was in his office in Montgomery, wheeling and dealing, or whatever he did.

As time went on and Bundy's attitude towards her worsened, she got to the stage that she didn't care where he went, or how long he stayed away, just so long as he kept away from her. She had been greatly disappointed that she had never been encouraged to have any meaningful input into the running and management of the household, or to take part in any activity around the ranch.

On a number of occasions, through sheer boredom, she had tried to involve herself. She was always met with a wall of courteous hostility. By and large, she was allowed the run of the house and rooms, so long as she didn't interfere. There was one exception. Bundy's study, a small room on the first floor, was kept permanently locked. To Selina there was a sinister fascination about this room. She was determined sooner or later to strip it of its secrets. She knew, however, that she would have to be careful. If Bundy caught her spying on him, he would turn very nasty, she knew that. She would have to bide her time.

Even though she was technically mistress of this beautiful mansion, she had already begun to feel like a prisoner in it. Bundy's treatment of her resembled that of a chattel rather than a

Six

living wife. Despite his obvious wealth, he kept her woefully short of money. He put no money into an account for her, and didn't allow her a checkbook. If she tried to run up bills in local shops, he refused to pay them. All this was a dreadful blow to money-loving Selina. In many respects she was financially worse off than during her Mississippi days. At least then she had been free to earn something working at the nightclub.

When she tackled him about it, Bundy flew into a rage, informing her she was better off than most, living in his beautiful house. When she told him she was going to seek work in Montgomery, he said no wife of his would ever work. The one concession Bundy was prepared to make was to allow her the use of a beat up old Dodge station wagon. It had a diesel engine, and as he had a diesel tank on the estate for his ranch vehicles, she was allowed to fill up from that. When he offered her this he was unaware that she was unable to drive. She had never owned a car in her life, but nothing would have made her tell him. Eventually Julius came to her rescue, helping her to master the art. The Dodge probably saved her from going mad. It represented a slice of freedom that otherwise she was not going to get.

Most days she would trundle into Montgomery to try to make friends. Even that was easier said than done. In bars and cafés she attempted to get into conversation with folk, but no one was prepared to be friendly, especially when she told them to whom she was married. This only served to heighten her general unease about Bundy.

Once again her fragile confidence plummeted. Was there to be no light at the end of the tunnel? Soon she found herself reverting to type, doing the rounds of the bars, chatting up folk who had had too much to drink and drinking too much herself. She would accept drinks from anyone who offered. She would do anything to blot out her unhappiness.

One night Julius didn't come home at all. He had taken to returning to the ranch later and later. Sometimes it was three or four in the morning by the time he got home. When Selina tackled him about this behavior, she was met with a surly wall of silence. The next day he didn't put in an appearance either. By the time Bundy returned late that night, Julius still hadn't turned up.

Selina told Bundy what had happened. She was worried. He shrugged his shoulders and switched on his uninterested expression. She pointed out that Julius was legally his stepson, and that he should be concerned about his welfare.

'Y'er wastin y'er time gal, he's an ill-reared whelp, an' you knows it. Ah really don' care if ah nevah sets eyes on him agin!' Bundy responded.

Selina's sorely tried temper flared. 'Has yah no compassion fer the chile?' she asked with passion.

'Not on yer sainted life! Poor white trash kid, bin on skid row fer a long while. You've no control ovah him, whaddya expect me tah do?' He then gave that high-pitched whinny she had grown to hate.

Deeply insulted, she could take no more. She rushed at him where he was standing with his back to the fireplace. 'How dare yah, Cyrus Bundy. Yah take that back, d'yah hear!'

An ugly expression appeared on Bundy's face. He reached for the pearl-handled revolver he kept in a holster at his side. Drawing it, he pointed it directly at her chest. 'Not one step further ma'am, d'yah hear?'

Selina recoiled in horror. His eyes meant business. 'Nevah do that tah me again woman,' he said with venom. 'Nevah question mah authority in mah own house. Do you heah?'

He took his time about replacing his revolver. For what seemed like an eternity they glared at each other, open hatred in their eyes.

Three days later Selina received a telephone call from the police. She was required at the station. They would give her no further information. She knew it must have something to do with Julius.

On the way into Montgomery, she cursed Bundy for the Southern bastard he was, and his total lack of interest in her and her son. It just wasn't right. After the recent row she felt that she

Six

had burnt her boats. So much hatred and resentment existed between them that there could be no going back. But why? Things had started off so well. What had gone wrong?

At the station, the duty sergeant informed Selina that Julius had been arrested for selling drugs. She was escorted down a corridor to a cell at the end. Julius was seated on the edge of a bed. He wore that defiant look she was beginning to know so well. It appeared he had held back on his identity for as long as he could. But, judging by the fresh bruising on his face, the Sheriff's men had broken him down. She rushed to him.

Nathan achieved top marks in his scholarship papers for the University of New York. He enrolled in his freshman year just before his seventeenth birthday, one of the youngest students ever to attend the university. He discovered that his principle tutor was to be Mayo Cleveland.

Within a short time it became obvious the two had a high mutual regard for the other. The seeds of that regard were sown that day in the library. Never before had Cleveland taught such a student. Nathan was so young, yet so capable and with such enormous potential. He was a pure joy to teach. Cleveland took infinite pains to ensure that his young protégé was given the very best instruction he was capable of giving. Already, privately, he was prophesying a great future for Nathan.

This uncanny alliance did not go unnoticed by others. On the one hand, the brilliant, ambitious lecturer, soon to be offered a professorship on the other, the equally brilliant and outstanding student. Each had a barely concealed fascination for the other. Some of the more cynical in the university world hinted at a sexual aspect to the relationship.

'Not such a pairing since Romulus and Remus...' someone said.

'Those two are complete intellectual soulmates. Odd, given the ten-year age difference,' others said.

The Chameleon Candidate

Selina was greatly shocked when confronted by Julius and what he'd been charged with. A good-time girl herself, she had never taken drugs. She was aware that drugs, and in particular people who pushed them, were taken just as seriously in the South as anywhere else. She knew too that judges had been encouraged to hand out severe sentences in the hope of deterring the younger generation.

The growing drug culture of the early sixties was having devastating consequences. A great number of major crimes were caused by drugs. Julius was still a young man, and Selina had visions of him being placed in Juvenile Detention for years. Worse still, he could find himself in an open prison for adults.

She knew it would be a useless exercise, but she needed to probe, to ask him questions. As she suspected, once she started, down came the shutters. He settled for gazing defiantly over her head into space, speaking not a word. The police case was that he had been caught in the act of selling heroin to other youngsters.

As she gazed at her son, she felt quite impotent. She couldn't help him if he did not talk to her. Her mind went back to her recent showdown with Bundy. Why had he turned against her? Why had he become so vicious? Just for the sake of it? What was she supposed to have done to him? She was still the same person he knew before he married her. But he was not the same. At least, he was not the person she thought she knew. He was not being straight with her. He had never been straight with her.

She glared at Julius, resentment showing in her expression. He hadn't spoken so far, he was unlikely to start a conversation now. She got up to go. Suddenly, as she moved to the door of the cell, it came to her. She had rejected Bundy. She had rejected him in the bedroom. Could that be what his behavior was all about?

It was all coming back to her. One night, several months previously, drunker and even more uncouth than usual, he had dropped his pajama bottoms and tried to squeeze his bulk into bed beside her. Disgusted, she rejected him out of hand, pushing him onto the floor.

Six

At the time she put the incident out of her mind. She assumed he had done the same, if he had remembered it in the first place. But now it seemed his memory had been all too clear.

For months she had been racking her brains for an explanation of his behavior. This must be it. But knowing, or surmising, all this didn't really help her now. If anything, it made things worse so far as Julius was concerned. She knew to her cost that Bundy, if not a particularly popular man, was a powerful one. If he chose, he could probably get the Sheriff to quash the charges against Julius. They were drinking buddies, and it was a first offence. But it was no good, Julius would have to take his medicine for being the stupid little shit he was. She would have to suffer too. She was ashamed of him.

And so Nathan fell under the spell of Mayo Cleveland. This mutual fascination was to last until Cleveland's untimely death.

Cleveland had qualified as a lawyer at twenty-one and obtained a lecturer's position at twenty-three. Now, at twenty-eight, he was offered the chair of the faculty of law. But he hesitated about taking it. Most folk couldn't understand it, but Nathan knew why. His political ambitions had taken over. Soon he was to put his name forward as a candidate for New York City Council. He would run on an independent ticket, his mandate geared to general humanitarian issues and care for the environment. What also made him of great interest to the electorate, especially the black population in New York, was his reputation as a Civil Rights lawyer. A fair deal for blacks was in the very vanguard of his agenda.

Nathan canvassed and worked enthusiastically for his friend as and when he could. He was by his side on the day he was elected. He was there to see him receive his robes and scroll during a dignified ceremony at City Hall, a beautiful, long, low building off Park Row, Broadway.

'Next stop the Senate!' Cleveland said, accepting Nathan's congratulatory handshake.

Soon afterwards, Cleveland set up office on the ground floor of an apartment block off Tenth Avenue. It was just around the corner from the Empire Diner, a favorite watering hole. It was a place where continental-style tables were set out permanently on the sidewalk, a hazard to all night revelers, who would trip over them while staggering homewards. As a result of his canvassing experience, it was a natural step for Nathan to help his friend with his new surgery and political constituency work.

Julius was allowed out on bail on his mother's own recognizance. The trial was set for one month's time. During the run up to the trial, the atmosphere at the ranch could have been cut with a knife. The small thread that had survived as a link in communication had now finally broken.

At the trial, or so Selina thought, the quality of information supplied by Julius was of sufficient value to allow the police to arrest a drugs dealer, Haile Mustapha. Mustapha was an Arab who'd been operating in Alabama since the mid-fifties. Because of this, and because it was a first offence, Julius received six months communal labor in a Junior Detention Center – suspended.

Selina broke down with relief at the word 'suspended'. Nevertheless, she understood the gravity of what Julius had done. His card was now stamped for all time. More disturbing was the thought that his life might well be in danger. He had grassed on his supplying dealer, a dangerous thing to do. Disgusted with him, Selina signed him out of the court. She pushed him into the Dodge and they bumped their way back to the ranch in silence.

Nathan, now eighteen, was over six feet tall, with dark, striking good looks. He had enough of his father's blood in him to give him all the pulling power he might have wanted with girls. Ironically he didn't want it. He was a young man with a mission, and, as yet, girls were no part of it, they only drained you and took your mind off more serious things. He knew he was not ready to enter into any serious emotional involvement. There was work to be done, lots of it.

Six

From time to time he did see girls. There was always a steady queue of them, ready at the drop of a hat to take his clothes off. He certainly wasn't into that, but he would drink coffee with one or another occasionally, or go for a walk in the park. Never one for small talk, or flirting, he would walk away if a girl got too serious.

One night Aunt Nessie awoke with a headache so severe she cried out for Nathan. Seeing her obvious distress, he telephoned the doctor immediately. Old doctor Viktor Mankewitch came at once. A Polish Jew and survivor from Auschwitz, he had set up in general practice in a house off Vesey Street soon after the war. He had been the Connor's doctor since they married. As he left the house the old man looked troubled. Next day he arranged for Aunt Nessie to see a specialist. A malignant brain tumor was found. She was hospitalized, but within days discharged. Nothing further could be done for her. Within three months, Aunt Nessie was dead.

Nathan, with the help of Mayo Cleveland, arranged her funeral, a quiet affair. She was buried in the graveyard of Grace Church, beside her beloved Vinnie.

For a while Nathan was inconsolable. His aunt had watched him grow to manhood, blossoming into a clever, ambitious law student. She had been his rock, guardian and surrogate mother ever since he'd been sent to New York as an insecure little boy. Aunt Nessie always knew he would go places. She was never done telling him so. She had been as proud of him as if he'd been her own. Now she was gone and it left a huge gap, one that would take a long time to fill.

During the anti-climax that inevitably followed Aunt Nessie's funeral, Nathan had time to wonder afresh what had happened to his family in the South. Apart from the obvious reasons, he wished to inform his mother of Nessie Connor's passing. Once more, in the absence of any other contact, he decided to write to the Reverend Sam McColgan. Perhaps by now the minister would have some news for him?

Within the week he received a letter. There was no news from

Alabama. The letter ended with a blessing and a wish that Nathan could find contentment and fulfillment in his life.

Disappointed once again at his mother's continued lack of interest in him, Nathan put all thoughts of her and Julius to the back of his mind. He had already received a very pleasant surprise, something quite unexpected. Aunt Nessie had left her apartment to him in her will. A roof over his head for the rest of his days!

He was still not earning serious money. A student not yet finished university, he would at best have been able to rent a poor quality place, or, like so many others, go into student accommodation. Even though he had been baptized and brought up in the Southern Baptist tradition, Nathan had spent his teenage years going to the Roman Catholic Church with Aunt Nessie, although he had never taken confession. Now he felt a need to revert to his own religion, promising himself that he would join the congregation of a suitable Baptist Church as soon as practicable. Each night he offered prayers asking for the repose of Nessie's soul, and now that he was alone in the world, a prayer that he would soon resume contact with the rest of his family.

Not for the first or last time, he plumbed the depths of loneliness. New York, no matter what the buzz might be, could be a very lonely place for a country boy without his guardian and, apart from Cleveland, no close friends. He had not intended even to think about his mother for a very long time but, as his low mood persisted, he felt forced to wonder about her. Had she retained her glamour? He remembered her as vibrant and vivacious. Was her new husband good to her? Were they happy together? How was Julius faring? Nathan remembered Julius as a resentful little rebel, quite capable of frightening him with his vicious ways. He began to feel the emptiness of separation all over again. How wrong and wasteful it was for families to be so completely torn apart, as his had been. So overpowering did these thoughts become, that once again he sat at his desk. This time he decided to write to the Sheriff in Montgomery, in the hope that Selina had reached her stated

Six

destination, and that the local police would have knowledge of her as Bundy's wife.

This time he had more luck. Within two weeks he received a letter giving details of her address. He began to feel better. At least someone had heard of her and, on the face of it, she was alive and well. Within an hour of receiving this letter, Nathan fired off another one. This time it was to his mother. She was destined never to receive it.

Relationships in the Bundy household had reached an all-time low. Bundy insisted that all mail coming to the house came directly to him for vetting. Normally that would not have been a problem. Most of the post was for him anyway. The procedure was that the post was left in the box at the top of the drive. Each morning Freestone, the butler, would empty the box and bring the contents straight to his master. Bundy saw the New York postmark on Nathan's letter, opened it, scanned it and then threw it in the fire.

If Selina had read the letter, she would have received an open invitation to come to New York. Nathan would have met her at the station and taken her back to the apartment. But, even if she had known, Selina couldn't have accepted. The harsh truth was that marrying Bundy had effectively destroyed her soul. She lived with fear and disappointment every day. She was destined never to know that Aunt Nessie had died.

Without having the advantage of reading Nathan's letter, Selina had a gut feeling that Nathan was doing well. She always knew that out of the three, he would be the one to make it. He was always different. She had told him so often enough in the old days, especially when she was annoyed with him, or embarrassed by his pious ways.

She had felt for some time that some motherly instinct deep inside her had helped her to make the decision to send him to New York - to give him a chance. The painful truth was, despite genuinely wishing Nathan well, she was suffering an occurrence of the old resentment towards her elder son. This was compounded by her present unhappiness. She was not yet ready to meet him, not by a long chalk.

Chapter Seven

Selina's fascination grew and grew about what Bundy found so important in his study that he felt the need to keep it permanently locked. She felt a desperate compulsion to find out what sinister secret lay beyond the door. She knew it was bound to be sinister if it had anything to do with him. No longer did she have a shred of loyalty left for this monster. She would have to be very careful.

The study door was secured with a Yale lock, and another lock lower down. Belt and braces, she thought – typical of the man. As Bundy was out most days for most of the time, his presence in the house would pose little problem. But she would have to be careful about the house staff. They mustn't find her or suspect her motives. She knew, despite the despicable way he treated them, that they would tell Bundy, even if only to keep themselves on his right side and, of course, to get her into trouble.

First she would have to get copies of the keys cut. She checked the Yale one to make out a number or code, but couldn't find anything. The one lower down also yielded nothing. She would have to rely on impressions only. She mashed up a candle, heated it, and took wax impressions of both locks. Barely finished, she heard a noise behind her. Startled, she turned. Julius was coming down the corridor towards her. Guiltily, she backed away from the door.

'Mah Julius, yah near scared me tuh death. Don' dare snuck up on me like that!' she said, her heart beating like a tom-tom in her chest.

Street-wise, he'd already guessed what she was doing. He laughed.

'Well, well, well! So yah wanna know what's behin' thet there door, Ma?'

Composing herself as best she could, she glared at him. It occurred to her that he too must have been curious. 'Mah little ole heart's just a flutterin! Don't do that agin!' She wagged her finger at him, playing for time.

'Good job it wasn't one of them niggah's downstairs, eh, Ma?' he said sarcastically.

She didn't answer. At first embarrassed at being caught in the act, she hesitated to tell him what she was doing. But as he already knew, she decided to take him into her confidence. They went into his bedroom and closed the door.

She took a long lingering look at him standing in front of her, the sun streaming through the window. Not for the first time, she thought how tall and handsome he was, and so very dark. She had always admired dark looks in a man. How in thunder Thaddeus could have ever thought for minute that he would have been capable of siring a child so beautiful, she would never understand.

She told him exactly what was on her mind. He laughed loud and long.

'Yah could'a spared yersel the trouble with the wax!' he said.

'Whaddya mean?'

'Sure and ah kin open any door in minutes!'

Briefly, she glared at him in horror. How on earth had he acquired such a skill? Then, remembering that he really was her street-wise son, she saw the funny side of it.

True to his boast, Julius had both locks cracked in ten minutes. The only instrument he needed was a small piece of wire. Adrenalin rushed through her veins at the very thought of what they might find. What it was to have such a clever son! She was beginning to forgive him for the drug incident. The very nature of this joint escapade was bringing them closer together.

Julius kept guard on the landing while she methodically searched the room. The drawers in the desk were unlocked. She rummaged through them. There was nothing of interest. Nor was there anything unusual in the filing cabinet by the window. The

Seven

only furniture left was a huge dark oak wardrobe, taking up a complete wall. It was locked. She called to Julius. Within seconds this door, too, was open.

Inside was what anyone might have expected to find in a man's wardrobe. There were suits, a selection of belts, fancy neckwear, boots – some spurred – and an array of hats.

Selina was about to close the door, when something white on a hanger at the far end caught her eye. She dragged it out, and then dropped it on the floor as if it was burning hot. The full dress kit of the Ku Klux Klan stared up at her, the ridiculous cone shaped headgear with two holes for eyes! Hand to mouth, she stifled the scream that formed in her throat.

Meanwhile, Julius had found a concealed drawer at the back of the wardrobe. He reached in and extracted a gold-colored metal object. Backing out with it he held it above his head.

'The fiery cross!' he exclaimed.

This was the symbol that had struck terror into Ku Klux Klan victims down the years. He shook it at Selina.

Horrified, she covered her eyes. 'Ah knowed it, ah jist knowed it! All along ah knew he was into some devilish evilness!' Distraught, she kicked the white uniform the length of the room as if it was some deadly snake.

Julius whistled through his teeth. 'Holy shit, so old Cyrus's a member of the Klan! I bet they don' know that downstairs!'

Selina was incapable of answering him.

Nathan was coming to the end of his university days. Even during his short time there, a great deal had happened on the Civil Rights front. The Movement had, by now, taken the whole of the country by the throat. Daily, more and more influential folk were joining the ranks. Many students from the North had already headed South to help. Medgar Evers, a highly respected black leader in Mississippi, had been murdered two years previously, in the same year that President Kennedy had been assassinated.

The Chameleon Candidate

That year Martin Luther King marched on Washington. A quarter of a million people gathered in peaceful brotherhood at the Lincoln Memorial to hear his famous 'I have a dream...' speech.

This was the turning point for the fortunes of the millions of black citizens in America. It was this march, more than any other event, that forced the government in Washington to listen to the black leaders, and to take stock of the plight of the people they represented.

In particular, the news from Nathan's home state of Mississippi was not good. Apart from the murder of Evers, three young Northern Civil Rights workers had been abducted and killed for attempting to investigate the burning of a black church.

Jack Kennedy was the first President to understand fully the enormous power of television for good or evil. After his death, Johnson inherited an insatiable demand by the viewing public to attempt to solve all the problems besetting the nation.

Without doubt, the two main issues were Civil Rights and Vietnam. Some of the televised material shown relating to Civil Rights was very disturbing. Viewers across the country saw attacks by police on peaceful demonstrators, culminating in one particularly dreadful incident. There were graphic shots of Alabama troopers, on horse and foot and armed with tear gas, assaulting peaceful marchers at both Selma and Petter's Bridge.

It was only during the summer before he died that Kennedy managed to get to grips with the flagrant defiance of federal authority by public officials, commonplace in the South. This defiance was clear in the behavior of a certain George Wallace, Governor of Alabama. Wallace's show of contempt for Washington brought federal bayonets onto the University of Alabama Campus at Tuscaloosa.

It was then Kennedy was forced to say, '...the fires of frustration and discord are burning in every city North and South. We face a moral crisis. It is time to act in Congress.'

Seven

Both Mayo Cleveland and Nathan followed these events closely. For a while, during the worst of the incidents, Nathan was tempted to head for Mississippi, there to help directly the fight for Civil Rights. But he was ultimately persuaded that Cleveland's need for him in New York was greater. Instead he joined the Northern Movement, working tirelessly for it.

In the South the main problems faced by the blacks were legal and constitutional. In the North, they had to deal with social and economic discrimination.

Being the kind of person he was, and from his background, Nathan had a great deal of empathy with the problems of Southern blacks, but in practice he was able to do little about it. He was better placed, however, to give practical help to the many black people in Cleveland's own constituency.

Now that he had won his seat on New York City Council, Cleveland was working to raise his profile. For some time, he had had his sights set on the Senate. Anything he could do to propel himself down that golden road, he would do. At the same time he would do it openly and honestly, through his day-to-day work and through the issues he believed passionately in. Top of the list was a fair deal for blacks. In this connection he found Nathan particularly useful.

Apart from his sensitive cleverness and general observational skills, Nathan had developed a very mature way of dealing with people. He was a young man with exactly the right background to deal sympathetically and knowledgeably with Cleveland's black constituents.

What Northern blacks desired most of all, now that the Civil Rights Train had well and truly left the station, was the conscious attention and respect of whites. Cleveland had long since tuned into this, so it wasn't long before even the black leaders in New York State were queuing up for his advice, and that of his young assistant.

The Chameleon Candidate

In the South, matters couldn't have been much worse than in Alabama. Since 1960 Civil Rights workers had been actively protesting in that State in particular. But what was causing Selina Bundy the gravest concern these days was her discovery that her husband was a member of the dreaded Ku Klux Klan. She knew well enough from her Mississippi days just how dreadfully cruel and unreasonable these people could be. Their habit of trial and summary execution on sometimes nothing more than a whim or rumor was terrifying and totally unacceptable to right-thinking folk.

The trouble was that there were a great many Southern folk, who, on the face of it, should have been right thinking, but were obviously not. People who, at best, turned a blind eye to such activities or, in many cases, actively condoned them. It was in such fruitful soil that these evil seeds were allowed to germinate and flourish. The very thought of the dreadful things Bundy and his associates must have involved themselves in, made Selina shudder all over. She wondered how many of the executions she had seen on television or read about he had been associated with. He must have black blood on his hands. So, her intuition of avoiding sexual intercourse from the start had been correct.

While she had been brought up poor white trash in poverty stricken Mississippi, Selina had to admit that she had no overpowering love for blacks. But she didn't have any great hatred for them either. Looking back, she could count numerous black people who had stretched out the hand of friendship to her.

In this regard she was unlike either of her sons. If she had been capable of thinking about it, she would probably have considered herself neutral, whereas Nathan was definitely a 'nigger lover'. She guessed that right now he would probably be sticking his superior nose into the growing Civil Rights business. That would be an extension of his attitude as a small boy. At the other end of the spectrum was Julius, with a full load of racist hatred bottled up inside him.

Seven

The discovery in the study now gave Selina an even worse psychological problem, if that were possible, in her attitude towards Bundy. She had no idea how she could face him at all. She would find it impossible to keep the deep-rooted feelings of loathing out of her eyes and expression. But she would have to try, at least for the present until she had worked out her future. Bundy was cunning like a fox. If he suspected she was spying on him, there would be no saving her. Above all, she needed time. Time to herself, time to think, time to plan.

That summer, Cleveland and Nathan began to forge a partnership to be part of the spearhead for the Northern Civil Rights Movement. At the same time, Cleveland was using this as a power base to help to pave the way for his next ambition – a seat in the Senate. Nathan worked with him for long hours, unselfishly, giving of himself as if he was the one trying to get elected.

Both were distressed to learn about James Meredith, the gutsy colored Air force veteran, who had succeeded in integrating the University of Mississippi in 1962. In continuing his good work, he set off that summer to march across Mississippi, in a one-man demonstration to point out that Mississippi blacks were still far from free. After only one day he was shot dead by a white man.

Selina was only just beginning to recover from the shock of discovering Bundy's sinister secret and pondering on the way ahead, when another disaster struck.

It was the beginning of the serious drug scene, linked inevitably to the folk singers of the time, such as Bob Dylan, Judy Collins, Joan Baez and Pete Seger.

In February of the previous year, Stanley's primitive acid speed factory in Berkeley, California was raided. But to no avail. The next month, he simply moved his whole operation to Los Angeles, where he went into production of lysergic acid monohydrate.

This signaled the beginning of drugs for the masses. Folk tuned into the illusion that '...chemistry could free human mind to spin through full cycle, from frenzied hope and bombastic prophecy to panic, paranoia and catastrophe...' In short, it was the era of the hippy and the hippy colony.

Tragically, for Selina, it was also the year that Julius walked out of her life to join just such a colony.

For some time, Julius had been unable to see any future for himself either with his mother, or Bundy. Expelled from school for unacceptable behavior, he spent most of his time either bumming around the ranch, where he was unwelcome, or sliding off into Montgomery. Just as with Bundy, Selina had no idea where he went, what he did, or whom he saw. Totally unable to reach him, she had a nasty feeling he could be into the drugs scene again.

One thing worried her in particular. He always seemed to have money in his pocket. When she probed him about it, he either wouldn't answer her, or else claimed that he'd been running errands for local shopkeepers. One day she lost her temper and emptied his pockets. She found over one hundred dollars. He explained that he'd found a job driving a delivery van for a grocery firm. When she asked the name of the firm, he was evasive. When she insisted, he told her to mind her own business. Then, one night he didn't come home.

Distraught, she knew something bad was up. She didn't know what to do. This time she was afraid to go to the police for fear of what they might be able to tell her.

After seven days with no contact with Julius, she was forced to contact the Sheriff's office. There was no trace. For many nights after that, Selina cried herself to sleep. She felt she had let Julius down, that he must have thought there was no hope for him with either Bundy or herself.

Once the situation had sunk in, Bundy took great pleasure in reminding her that Julius was no longer a minor. He could go where he liked, when he liked, so long as he did not break the law.

Inside herself Selina knew this was exactly what he was doing –

Seven

breaking the law.

Two months to the day after he disappeared, just when she was beginning to lose all hope of ever seeing him again, word filtered through that Julius had been spotted in a hippy colony in Berkeley. Due to the fact he was already on police records, the identification was made by the Californian police.

When tackled, Julius told them in no uncertain terms to clear off. He had severed all connections with his family. He never wanted to see his mother or stepfather again. He certainly had no intention of ever returning to Montgomery.

When this was relayed to Selina she was broken hearted. She knew that he meant what he said. What sort of a dreadful nightmare was her life turning into? She couldn't have done worse if they had all stayed in Mississippi.

Once more she began to plot to leave Bundy. This time she would have to mean business. She would go just as soon as she could. With absolutely no happiness, or quality of life, or prospect of any, what was the point of staying to be his punch bag?

In her distress, she started thinking about Nathan. This time she really would write to him. She wrote care of Aunt Nessie's address, posting the letter personally in Montgomery. Now she would have to be prepared to set aside her pride.

The letter was full of bad spellings, and was painfully short, revealing just a hint of her unhappiness with Bundy. She didn't mention anything about Julius's disappearance. She ended by hoping that he had found happiness in his new life. As a postscript, she scratched a few words of gratitude to Aunt Nessie.

Nathan was delighted to receive the letter. It was the first one his mother had ever written to him. He replied without delay, explaining that he had found difficulty in obtaining her address, but that he had written before. Perhaps she had not got that letter? He told her the sad news of Aunt Nessie's passing, and that she had left the apartment to him. He sketched out his progress in life, explaining that he was now in his final year at university, and hoping to qualify as a lawyer.

Selina read and re-read the letter. She marveled that she had such a son, one who could use the most beautiful words, a son whose handwriting was so well formed and clear. She could hardly write at all, let alone spell accurately. She was sad to hear about Nessie, but still glad to hear from Nathan. It helped to give her the emotional lift she was so desperate for.
She realized that Bundy must have destroyed his first letter. It was only because she was expecting this one that she received it at all. She had the postman deliver it to her own hand.
After some reflection, and mainly because Nathan's letter to her had been so open and friendly, she decided to open her heart to him. She had bottled things up long enough. The time had come to confide in someone. Again she wrote. This time she sketched out, in as much detail as she was capable, her life since the parting of the ways all those years ago. She had to admit that she had made a dreadful mistake in marrying Bundy, that he was not the man she thought he was. She told Nathan of her present fear of him, about his meanness. She decided to hold back, for the present, about his Ku Klux Klan links. She mentioned that his brother Julius had been a real handful. He'd never really settled down in Alabama. She hinted he'd had a brush with the law, but couldn't bring herself to mention drugs. She certainly couldn't bring herself to tell him that Julius had effectively closed her out of his life, that he was a drop out, living in another state, both figuratively and literally.
Nathan responded speedily to this second, equally welcome letter. Despite her apparent lack of interest in him over the years, his heart went out to her now. It was obvious that she had gotten a raw deal. Little did he know how raw. He begged her to come to New York to stay awhile. She could have Aunt Nessie's room. She could even bring Julius with her. He would send the tickets.

Seven

But, even though she had plucked up courage to make contact with him, she knew in her heart she couldn't cope with New York. She was still too ashamed to face him. Perhaps another time?

Chapter Eight

Nathan qualified as a lawyer specializing in Civil Rights work. Things were moving fast on the Civil Rights front. Martin Luther King had asked Jesse Jackson, freshly into the national spotlight, to head up Operation Breadbasket. This was the vitally important economic branch of the Southern Christian Leadership Conference.

Lyndon Johnson was struggling to hold together his doomed administration. Two years previously he had made the terminally grave error of escalating the war in Vietnam, in the hope of bringing it to a speedy conclusion. It had the exact opposite effect, and was to finish him as president. It was still very much the era of the hippy, as highlighted by the Monterey Festival, and all that went on there.

There was also the gathering of the tribes at Golden Gate Park. Thousands of the faithful, in a state of deep hallucination, watched the sun set over the Pacific, while poet Alan Ginsberg blew on a ram's horn and recited appropriate prose.

Selina was relieved to hear from Nathan. Having at long last established the link, she was anxious to continue with it. She replied, telling him about her feelings regarding New York, thanking him for his invitation, but declining it. She hoped he would understand.

Further news filtered through about Julius. He had been seen at the gathering at Golden Gate Park. He had grown a long beard and was practically unrecognizable.

At this time, Selina began to feel that things were finally coming to a head with Bundy. His attitude was now one of permanent

Eight

open hostility. Ever since the night she rejected him in the bedroom, he had not tried again. Soon after that she had her own room. One day she returned from town to find the servants moving her things out of the master bedroom into a smaller room at the front of the house. When she asked what was going on, she was informed it was on Bundy's instructions. Initially, she was both pleased and relieved. But on reflection, she felt this act by him was the beginning of the end. For all intents and purposes it was then he had put her out of his life. She resented that he made her feel like a frightened, trapped animal in the very house she was supposed to be mistress of. It couldn't go on much longer. She had to escape, to start again somewhere, no matter how distasteful that thought was. But where?

She had no other home, no money, no relations. There was not a single person that she could call a friend in the whole of Alabama. Even in her distressed state she couldn't consider the thought of going back to Idle Winds. That would be a backward step, not one to be taken under any circumstances. Nathan was the only person she had contact with these days, and she had already made the decision not to go to New York.

Bundy's very presence inhibited all her thought processes. He had really begun to terrify her, and although she never lacked courage in the old days, she was now greatly disadvantaged, being on her own in the big house, without even Julius to back her. The truth was she was in a total vacuum, unable to think clearly. Bundy had never treated her like a wife, except during the first few weeks of their marriage. Then the rot had set in.

She wasn't a servant, he had plenty of those. She wasn't a housekeeper, he had a Louisiana colored woman called Victoria for that. She did the ordering, catering and supervision of meals, which were cooked by the young Cajun chef Claud, who rarely spoke, and appeared terrified of Bundy.

She certainly wasn't a companion. Bundy was hardly ever at home, and when he was, he didn't speak to her. He didn't allow her to become involved in anything. His whole attitude was totally dismissive. There was no place for her in his life. But she couldn't afford to let him away so easily. If she just walked out, as every fiber in her body urged her to do, he would have the perfect excuse to cut her off without a dime.

If she had been able to make friends with any of the staff, she might have been able to develop a power base. That had not been possible. She had tried. For sure, they were all courteous enough, but remote, too, not giving an inch of themselves. It was almost as if Bundy had programmed them.

For a time she flirted with the idea of trying to divorce him on the grounds of cruelty. But she soon rejected that idea. He was a powerful, ruthless man who would soon rally around him a team of lawyers who could blow any piddling thing she could say out of the water.

In her torment, her mind chugged on. She pondered on the thought of catching him out in some illegal act. A Ku Klux Klan escapade, for example. Surely that would strengthen her case against him?

Her distraught mind focused on this one possible solution to her problems. She knew she had a strong case against him if only she could get someone to listen. It would have to be something really incriminating, something he could not deny, something the police could not ignore.

It was all very well saying her husband was a member of the Ku Klux Klan, that he had the incriminating uniform. But whom could she tell? Who would be interested? Who would actually tackle Bundy? No one! Absolutely goddamn nobody!

But if she was successful, then all kinds of doors would open. She would have access to money, to a place of her own. Maybe she would even be able to get the family together again. She could go after Julius. Then she would have something to offer him. Perhaps she could persuade Nathan to set up a law practice in the South? All these wild thoughts raged around her poor distraught mind.

Eight

Her mind, obsessed now, worked on. She recalled that within the past few months the newspapers had reported a particularly brutal murder in the district. It had all the hallmarks of a Ku Klux Klan killing, they said. A young white man, a ranch hand, had been labeled 'nigger lover'. His body was found in a field a few miles south of the ranch. She wondered if Bundy had been involved. But exactly how to incriminate him? This was the problem that occupied Selina's every waking moment.

Time and again, she wondered why a man such as he, obviously a serious nigger hater, could bring himself to employ so many coloreds in his household – to actually offer them paid employment. The more she thought about it, the more she came to realize that it was typical of him, typical of his general craftiness, his skill at self-protection. It was all a ruse to throw folk off the scent. Perhaps it was the accepted thing for Southern ranchers to do? She didn't know. After all, it was really a form of latter day slavery. Especially in his case, given the way he treated his staff!

A plan began to shape up in her mind, a dangerous, crazy plan. Selina had already figured the only way she was going to get the evidence she so desperately needed was to wait until Bundy was into his next Ku Klux Klan contract. Once she had established this, she would follow him with a camera and a tape recorder on the off chance that sometime during the assignment he would remove his headgear. Then he would be photographed. The tape recorder was to record his voice. She had seen on television that this sort of evidence could be admissible in court. If she pulled it off, that would be her evidence – indisputable evidence.

She knew where to get the camera and tape recorder. Julius had left both in his room. A fanatical Bob Dylan fan, he had used the tape recorder to tape his records. Obviously he had little need of either when he embarked on his new life.

Selina wished she knew a local journalist, someone to whom she could feed the story, someone who could back her with resources. Above all, she needed a person whom she could trust completely.

The Chameleon Candidate

That would make life so much easier. But there was no such person in her life. So, as usual, she found herself alone and operating with little confidence in her own ability to carry the project through.

She wished with all her heart that Julius would come back. For all his wild and troublesome ways, he was a strong young man. He would have helped and protected her. He had never been afraid of Bundy, not the way she was.

From this point on Selina kept her ear as close to the ground as she dared. She listened out around the ranch, but more especially in Montgomery, in pubs, cafés and clubs, anywhere where people congregated to socialize. She was desperate to garner any scrap of information that might alert her to a possible forthcoming Klan killing.

She had gotten to know some of the barmen reasonably well as a customer coming in and out, but not well enough to trust with her mission.

She knew that Alabama was probably the worst State in the whole of the South to attempt to break through the Ku Klux Klan blanket of fear. Soon she realized that she dare not broach the subject at all. If she picked the wrong person, it wouldn't be long before Bundy heard about it. It would be equally fruitless to question black residents. They would be too frightened to open up.

But it wasn't long before her lonely determination began to pay off. One night in Hank's Place, as she sat at the bar, three people entered. They sat at a table close to her. Something about them alerted her. All had hard fascist faces. Two were in their late thirties, one dark, one fair. The third, a huge man with a bald head, was about Bundy's own age.

The bald man ordered bourbon, and they sat huddled, acting the role of conspirators. Selina tuned in. She did this under the guise of pretending to be drunk. She had perfected the trick in the nightclub in Mississippi over the years.

The fair one said, 'Damn niggah, got it commin tah him!'

Baldy said one letter, 'K.'

Eight

The others nodded, straightened up and gazed about in a defensive way. The dark one ordered another round of drinks.

Selina knew she had struck gold! She continued with her drunk act, sprawled across the top of the bar, for all intents and purposes past any kind of comprehension. Again the conspirators bent in urgent discussion.

She was able to pick out certain words only. But it was enough. If she was right, they were talking about a contract freshly taken out on a Negro, a Civil Rights activist, named Tandy. The execution was to be on Saturday night – four nights away! Tandy was to be taken from his home, driven to the execution site, and given the works.

The three lingered at the table for another hour. By now the conversation had turned to mundane matters. Selina was forced to stay too. She longed for a drink, but deemed it too dangerous to ask. If they saw she was able to do that, then she could also be capable of overhearing them.

Back at the ranch she made her plans. Next day, she took the camera and tape recorder from Julius's room, checking that they were both loaded and working. Then she went into town and hired a van for Saturday. Having no money to pay for this, she arranged for the account to be sent to Bundy.

Saturday arrived. She'd reckoned on Bundy going out after breakfast, as usual. He did, but without his huge briefcase, the one in which she suspected he carried his execution kit. As soon as his car disappeared down the drive, she put her own plan into action. She drove her Dodge into town, returning within the hour in the hired van, parking it in the trees at the edge of the driveway. At that point it couldn't be seen from the house, but allowed her a view of the drive.

There she waited in the van, nerves as tight as a bunch of twisted wires. She knew she couldn't follow Bundy in the pink Dodge. She wouldn't get ten yards doing that. But she had to follow him to the execution site; it was the only way she would know where it was.

She needed transport to do it, hence the hired van.

Late in the afternoon, she heard Bundy's car scrunching the gravel on the drive. Moments later he drove past her hiding place. She strained her eyes and saw his bulk entering the front door. Within ten minutes he came out again, carrying his briefcase.

As soon as his Pontiac passed her again, she started the engine of the van and cautiously nosed out onto the driveway. She was just in time to see his car sweep out of the main entrance onto the highway and head south. She gave chase, accelerating onto the highway on his tail.

Driving fast and well – Julius had done a good job in teaching her – Selina closed on Bundy. He didn't look around, and even if he did see the van in his rearview mirror, he should have no reason to suspect he was being followed. To assist her disguise, she wore dark glasses and a headscarf.

After fifteen minutes driving, Selina keeping him in view all the time, Bundy suddenly turned sharply off the highway onto a dirt road. She was not expecting this and overshot. She pulled onto the hard shoulder and waited several minutes before turning back.

She was becoming very nervous. It was time to enter the lion's den. If Bundy's suspicions had been aroused about being followed, these would be confirmed if she was seen following him off the highway.

The road was in poor condition and full of potholes. She drove for several minutes, gingerly negotiating several gaping holes. She rounded a corner and came to the edge of a field. There were cars parked, she counted seven. Swiftly she reversed back, praying that no other car would come in behind her, or that she had been seen from the front.

She pulled the van off to her left, into a rough area behind a small hill. Out of the van, creeping on all fours through the thick grass surrounding the field, she reached the edge of the field. Her watch said 9.30 pm. The light was beginning to leave the sky.

From her vantage point she spotted a small wooden hut at the far

Eight

end of the field. Perhaps that's where the action is, she thought.

She waited, crouched deep in the grass for half an hour, while the sky darkened. Nothing stirred. Silently, stealthily, she moved towards the hut, keeping under cover as much as she could.

Finally, she was at the rear. She pressed her ear to the wooden paneling. She could hear the drone of voices, but not what was being said. She looked up and saw a small window to her left. She longed for a quick peek, but deemed it too dangerous. Her pulse was racing. The hut, little more than a large box, was about twenty feet long. Judging by the number of cars, it must be packed, she thought.

Selina was considering her next move, when suddenly the door burst open. She could hear people coming out. She froze. All of a sudden, she became very afraid. She began to tremble violently. Only when she felt sure that the hut must be empty, did she raise herself to the window and look in. It was deserted.

She dragged herself to the corner to allow her to see into the field beyond. What she saw made her gasp with fear.

In the field she counted eight figures standing in a circle. They were all dressed in Klan uniforms. In the center was a struggling figure. She strained her eyes to see a black man being bound and gagged. Two people were hammering a stake into the ground. Others closed in, carrying bundles in their arms. They threw them to the ground.

'My God, it's brushwood! They're goin ta burn him alive!' Selina said aloud, forgetting the danger she was in. She watched as they strapped the unfortunate victim to the stake. Then the wood was set alight.

As soon as the flames rose the circle of men began their devilish chant as they moved slowly around the stake. In turn, as they passed in front of the victim, they set fire to wooden crosses, holding them high above their heads.

By now the skyline was red with the flames from the fire, as more and more wood was piled around the base. Even from her position several hundred meters away, Selina could hear the muffled cries coming from the black man.

'Inhuman pigs!' she spat into the grass in her disgust.

By now it was sufficiently dark to risk getting closer. She realized that the tape recorder would be of little use now, so she tossed it into the long grass. But the camera certainly would be useful. She moved forward and across, coming in from the flank. She must get as close as she could.

A mixture of fear and adrenalin filled her veins as she crept closer. She hoped that the roar and crackle of the fire, together with the general excitement of the execution, would allow her to take the pictures unseen.

She had already snapped Bundy's car and his number plate at the entrance to the field. Quite by chance, he had parked it beside an unusual shaped mound. She felt this could be identified when she presented her evidence.

Now, if she could just get a shot of him without his hood! She moved in for her action shots. She pointed the camera in the general direction of the nightmarish scene and pressed the button. The flash flared.

'Oh my God!' Selina gasped. She didn't realize it would be so bright! She prayed the flash would be lost in the light coming from the fire. Another one for luck. Again the flash exploded. One final one! This time her luck ran out.

Shouts! Figures broke away from the circle and ran towards her. They were swearing. Selina panicked, turned and ran, dropping the camera. She heard the shot. She felt a searing pain in the back, then nothing. Selina Beauregarde pitched forward in the grass, dead.

Chapter Nine

It was Bundy himself who had fired the shot, the shot that killed his own wife.

Moments after they saw the camera flash, he and two others reached the spot where Selina's body lay, a poor pathetic crumpled heap in the grass. They whipped off their hoods to investigate. If Selina had been alive she would not only have recognized her own husband, but the other two younger men she had seen in the bar a few days before.

Bundy got there first. Callously, he turned the body with his foot.

'Sweet Jesus!' he said, amazed. He checked for signs of life. There were none. Selina had been dead by the time she hit the ground.

The others arrived. One said, 'Christ, surely that's...'

'Yeah Hank, that's mah wife. Stupid bitch! That'll teach her ta meddle in mah affairs!' His face registered shock, but precious little compassion. Shock, because he had not known Selina had tailed him to the field.

Despite their ruthless treatment of the Negro Tandy, the younger men were visibly shaken by Bundy's lack of response to what he'd done. Calmly, Bundy retrieved the camera that had fallen from Selina's hand. He opened it, extracted the film, and with a powerful heave of his arm, sent the empty camera hurtling high into the air, to land in thick scrub. Returning to the fire, he threw the film – the film Selina had given her life for – into the embers.

If Bundy had been shocked, as even he must have been, the effects wore off quickly enough. In a steady voice he told the others what had happened. Some of them, still hyped up over the execution of Tandy, were unaware that anyone had been shot, let alone

Bundy's own wife. Despite the dreadful business they had just finished, disturbed faces were to be seen once the headgear came off.

In his cold fashion, Bundy swore them to secrecy. He had every reason to believe they would respect this. He knew if they mentioned Selina's murder that would tie them in with the execution of Tandy.

The next problem was to hide the body. Would they help him? He broached the subject with some caution. Men of the world they might be, but they were under no illusion about what he was asking. Accessory to murder was a capital offence, in their minds a much more threatening proposition when it involved a white woman.

Three agreed to help. They carried Selina's body to Bundy's car, and in the process, discovered the white van. Bundy realized that this was the vehicle Selina had used to follow him. They set the body in the trunk. One of them produced a spade.

'Ah don't want it back, Cyrus!'

They deliberated about what to do with the van, finally deciding to drive it out onto the hard shoulder of the highway. Selina had left the keys in the ignition, so they locked it and threw them away. They reasoned that with any luck the traffic police would consider it was an ordinary breakdown.

It did occur to Bundy as he drove off alone that even he had asked a great deal of his colleagues, expecting them to act as accessories. Still, it was done now, and he wasn't a man to allow himself to be burdened by matters of conscience. Instead he said out aloud, 'Fuckin stupid bitch. Now see what you've made me do, all yer own fuckin' fault!'

He did not drive west towards the ranch, instead he headed south. He drove for ten miles, then took a turn to the left. He was unfamiliar with the countryside, but it appeared to be heavily wooded, admirable for his purpose.

He drove to the edge of a dense pine forest, and extinguished his

Nine

headlights. Then, spade in hand, he penetrated the forest for some two hundred yards. By the light of a torch he dug as if his life depended on it. Three quarters of an hour later, he had dug a grave sufficiently deep to hide Selina's body. Returning to the car, he opened the trunk, hauled the body out and dragged it to the edge of the grave. With a final heave, it rolled into the hole. Another fifteen minutes were spent erasing all traces of freshly dug soil. By now his breathing was hard and labored, his face puce from such unaccustomed activity.

Only then did he set off for the ranch. The clock in the dashboard said seven minutes past midnight. On the way back he stopped on a bridge to hurl the spade over the parapet into the fast flowing waters of the Tombigee River.

Later that day, Bundy informed his staff that his wife had left him. She had told him she was returning to her native Mississippi. She would not be back. He did not know her address. That evening he gathered together all Selina's clothes and jewelry, consigning them to the incinerator in the basement.

The repercussions of Selina's death were slow to surface, but surface they did. Almost six months to the day after the murder, a hunting dog out with its master dug up her grave.

As she had been so very isolated in her life with Bundy, there were few folk around to inquire about Selina. This suited Bundy down to the ground. He had done an excellent job of virtually eradicating her personality. Her letters to Nathan had been late in starting, then intermittent; as a result it would be some time before he suspected anything was wrong.

So, in the aftermath of her murder, a deadly silence settled over everything pertaining to Selina. It was as if she'd never existed.

In the nature of things in slow moving Alabama, especially where the colored population was concerned, an inquest was eventually held on the unfortunate Tandy. Like Selina, he appeared to have no family to mourn his passing. The verdict was predictable for an Alabama court of the time, murder by person or persons unknown. The police file was closed with unseemly haste, never to be re-opened.

Just as slowly was the body, discovered by the hunting dog, finally identified as that of Selina Bundy. Bundy had helped to delay identification by removing all jewelry and rings and burying her in her underclothes.

Despite these precautions, a connection was made to Bundy. He told the police little more than he'd already told his staff. His wife had left him by walking out of the house one day, telling him she was leaving him. She was returning to Mississippi, she was homesick for her kin there. No, he didn't know who they were, or where they lived. She had never discussed them with him.

He showed them her empty wardrobes. She had taken everything with her. He admitted she had been unhappy and restless for some time before she left, despite all he had done for her. Yes, she had been upset by the disappearance of her son. She had taken it very badly. Yes, he admitted to the occasional verbal row. No, he certainly never raised his fist to her in his life. No, he had no idea who would have wanted to murder her. So far as he knew, she didn't have an enemy in the world. When he had need to be, Cyrus Bundy was the most convincing of men.

Again the whole matter was buttoned up. This time there was an open verdict, despite the fact that the cause of death was a bullet wound in the back. Bundy had Selina's body re-buried in the municipal cemetery in Montgomery.

Time went by, and Nathan had begun to worry. He had received no word from Selina for seven months, which was a long time even by her standards. He knew now that life with Bundy – '...with them dreadful cruel eyes, colder than the Mississippi in January...' she once wrote him, was far from happy. But what could have happened? Where was Julius, and what was he up to?

Richard Nixon had been elected President in November of the previous year, 1968, and was due for inauguration in January. He

Nine

had inherited a poisoned chalice from Lyndon Johnson, the responsibility for ending the war in Vietnam. This war had finished Johnson and would threaten to de-rail his successor during the early days of his administration.

Twenty-three now, Nathan had already qualified as a lawyer. His friend Mayo Cleveland found him a position as a junior attorney in the law firm of Marquis and Goldstein, off Tenth Avenue. This firm specialized in Civil Rights work.

That whole year passed peacefully enough for Nathan, working hard at his new job. He made many useful contacts and impressed colleagues and clients alike with his mature perception of problems, and his knowledge and skill in solving them.

As the year turned, the authorities began to breath a sigh of relief, in so far that the worst of the hippy phase appeared to be over. In a number of areas colonies had already broken up. Many of the older, more serious fun seekers, were horrified at what bad publicity had done for their cult. Consequently, lock, stock and barrel, they had moved out of hippy ghettoes, to experiment alone on their less instant paths to truth. Woodstock was still to come. It looked very much like the last great acid trip of the sixties was, for all intents and purposes, shaking down on its last legs.

Ironically, it was Julius, and not Nathan, who was the first to discover the dreadful news of their mother's death. Somewhere along the line he had seen the light and began to reject the way of life that had been his for over two years. During that time he had moved from Berkeley to Los Angeles, where he had been living with hundreds of other like-minded youngsters in a commune.

Twice he had overdosed on heroin. The second time, he had OD'd so badly that he had been rushed to hospital. For a crucial forty-eight hours he was within an ace of death. Finally, he did pull through, and when he opened his eyes from the coma, he was a new man. It was the beginning of his rejection of all he had become. The experience had sown in him a strong determination

The Chameleon Candidate

to come off drugs once and for all. He needed to try to do something better with his life.

Within three weeks he was discharged from The Craig Memorial Hospital, the hospital that had saved his life, and hadn't charged him a dime.

That day he began his hitch-hike back to Montgomery. He knew he had fences to repair with his mother. Perhaps even the ogre Bundy could be seen through different eyes now? He arrived back in Montgomery within the week, reaching the ranch late one afternoon. Freestone opened the door. Julius inquired about his mother and stepfather. Bundy was out. Freestone didn't answer immediately regarding Selina. Julius asked again, thinking the old man had not heard him properly.

But Freestone had heard. He was merely taking his time about conveying the dreadful news of her death. When he did tell him, Julius was unable to take it in. When he finally did, he quizzed the butler for more information. But Freestone shrugged his shoulders, shook his head and walked back to the kitchen. He knew nothing more, he couldn't help him.

Julius mounted the stairs to the room that used to be his bedroom. He sat on the bed with his head in his hands. He had to think.

A mixture of emotions sped through his system as he tried to make sense of this bolt from the blue. But one thing did not alter as he thought the matter through. He was already convinced that Bundy must have had a hand in his mother's death. He would await his return and confront him.

He had lost his appetite, so had no desire to go downstairs in search of food. He had no possessions other than the clothes he came back in. He had exactly five dollars in his pocket. He passed the time scouring the drawers in the room checking to see what was left of his past life. There was nothing. Someone had removed everything.

He was certainly beginning his new life from scratch.

Nine

About midnight he heard the sound of a car engine revving hard. He looked out of the window to see Bundy's huge white Pontiac screeching up to the front door. Doors slammed. Doors opened. There were curses and heavy breathing. The master of the house had returned the worse for drink. Surprise, surprise, Julius thought.

In the hall Freestone tried to warn his master of Julius's return, but he was brushed aside. Making a great deal of noise, Bundy staggered up the stairs heading for his bedroom.

Julius waited till he heard the door slam, then went in search of him. He flung open the door. Bundy was seated on the bed, his head bent. He was very drunk. He looked up. His jaw went slack.

'What the hell yah doin' here, young mongrel?' His words were slurred.

But Julius, the reformed Julius, the older and wiser Julius, was in no mood to take any more insults from this monster who had treated his mother so badly. He couldn't forget that Bundy was the main reason he'd left and got into trouble in the first place.

Julius waded straight in. He tackled Bundy about Selina's death. 'I bet you had a hand in it, Cyrus. Admit it, yah ole bastard!'

Unprepared for this, Bundy did his usual blustering act, sticking to the story he'd already told the police.

'Yer a liar. Ma wouldn't go back tuh Mississippi. Yah knows that, there was nothin' there fer her!' Julius raised his voice in accusation.

Speaking slowly and as deliberately as his drunken state would allow, Bundy reiterated the circumstances of Selina's disappearance. She'd had words with him and had walked out of the house, taking her belongings in a suitcase. He'd watched her walking down the driveway. She had told him she was headed for Mississippi and she wouldn't be back. That was the last he ever saw of her. Six months later the police contacted him to tell him they'd found a body. They had reason to suspect it was Selina's. He was asked to identify it. That was all he knew.

'Yer lyin' Bundy, yer a damn cotton pickin' liar!' shouted Julius.

Bundy made to strike him, but thought better of it. Instead he settled for heaving himself off the bed, lurching towards Julius like a huge grizzly bear and, by sheer brute force, pushed him out the door.

At daylight, Julius left the ranch. He couldn't abide to spend one more moment under Bundy's roof. He hitched a lift into Montgomery and spent the rest of the day seeking work. He was lucky, by the end of the day he had found a job as a delivery boy for a grocery store. A bicycle went with it.

With the prospect of having some money in his pocket soon, he booked into a youth hostel. The room was tiny but it was clean.

That night he lay in bed and thought. He could have stolen money from Bundy. He knew where it was kept, in a safe in the dining room at the ranch. He could have cracked the combination in no time. That was what he would have done in the old days. But now he was not prepared to take anything from someone he detested.

Next day, in between deliveries, he took time out to talk with the police and some of the staff in the local bars. Nobody was saying very much, but the little they did say only helped to confirm his suspicions about Bundy. He was convinced it had something to do with the Klan. He learnt about the Negro Tandy, and the date of his execution – the very same day that Selina disappeared.

Sleep was beyond him, his mind was too active. He began to think about the ranch and his bedroom. What had happened to his belongings? He did a mental inventory of what had been in his room, in his drawers: clothes, shoes, records... records! Yes, that was it, his tape recorder, and his camera. His mother knew they were there, had she used them in some way? She was desperate to get away from Bundy, but she had no money. She needed a divorce with a proper financial settlement. But he wouldn't give it to her. How could she force him to give her money?

He was beginning to get a mental picture. What was the most

Nine

damaging thing she could do to him? Of course! Incriminating evidence of his involvement with the Ku Klux Klan would have provided her ticket out.

It was all beginning to slot into place. A contract had been out on Tandy, Selina had found out and tailed Bundy to the execution site armed with his camera and tape recorder in a vain attempt to obtain evidence she could use to get her divorce. She had been found out and Bundy had killed her to keep her quiet! It all fitted.

By now he was upright on the bed, huge gouts of sweat standing out on his forehead. He would have to fill in the details, but he was convinced that was the outline of what had happened.

The next evening, after his delivery run, he hitched a lift to the execution site. He knew where it was because he had read it in the newspapers. He found the field and the wooden hut, which was locked. More importantly, he noted the ring of scorched grass, not yet grown back, indicating the ferocity of the fire. He saw the hole where the stake had been. He even found pieces of brushwood lying around the area. These, he presumed, had been used to build the fire. All other evidence had been removed.

On his hands and knees, he searched the long grass where poor Selina had hidden prior to her murder. He was about to give up, when he saw something glint in the setting rays of the sun. He moved closer. It was a camera lens! He lifted the camera carefully by the strap, remembering about fingerprints. He examined it closely. It was his own, he knew by some marks on the casing. There was no film in it. He searched for the tape recorder, but there was no sign of it.

Next day, after work, he began to ask more questions. This time he was in earnest. But still nobody was talking. He would have to prove it himself, and until he did, he had no intention of leaving Montgomery.

He worked out a plan. If he could find Bundy's fingerprints on the camera, then this, together with the other circumstantial evidence that was stacked against him, might persuade the authorities to re-open the case.

The weakness of this was that it was his word against Bundy's. He had no witness to confirm that he had found the camera at the execution site.

Days went by and he thought of little else but how to get even with Bundy. Relentlessly, he would go over and over in his mind the sequence of events he thought must have taken place. He went to the local newspaper office on a number of occasions, reading and re-reading every word that was written about the two crimes, fixing dates and times in his mind.

Something was bothering him. There was a piece of the jigsaw missing. It was something to do with graves. Selina's body had been found in a pine forest, in a grave about six feet deep. In a grave about six feet deep! Who had dug it? Bundy? What had he dug it with?

A spade! If he could find that spade and link it to the crime, he would have his case made! He had never seen Bundy use a spade. There were probably spades about the ranch, but he had never seen any. It was not something Bundy would carry around with him in the trunk of his car in the normal way. He almost certainly would not have had it the night of the murder, because, according to Julius' theory, the crime had not been premeditated.

He assumed, correctly, that Bundy, being the loner he was, had dug the grave himself. Someone, therefore, must have given him the spade. One of the other conspirators? Nothing but a sharp spade could have dug a grave six feet deep. Julius rejected the idea that Bundy would have left the spade in his car after the burial. It would have meant he would have had to get rid of it around the ranch, and that would have been far too dangerous.

That left two possibilities. The spade could have been hidden in the forest near the grave. That seemed unlikely, the police had combed the area, and there was no report of a spade. Or, Bundy could have got rid of it somewhere between the forest and the ranch.

Nine

Julius obtained a large-scale map of the area where Selina had been found. That evening he studied it closely. He was not sure what he was looking for, except that it was somewhere to hide a spade. Of course, a river! The Tombigbee River, it was on Bundy's route home. The map showed a road bridge over the river, some six miles from the edge of the forest.

That weekend, he hired a motorcycle and set off for the bridge over the Tombigbee River. He tried to put himself in Bundy's shoes, a big man with huge arms, he would be able to hurl a spade a long way from the parapet of the bridge. He worked out what he considered to be an approximation of Bundy's aim, then went down to the river bank.

The Tombigbee, not as vast as the Mississippi, was nevertheless a sizeable river and fast flowing. He gazed into its murky depths for a while, seeking inspiration. Always a strong swimmer, self-taught from Mississippi days, he decided the only way of locating the spade, assuming it was there at all, was to dive and stay under for as long as he could.

He had no way of knowing what state the river bottom was in. Perhaps it would be so silted up that he would be unable to see anything. But it was fast flowing, not sluggish and sedate like the Mississippi, so there was just a chance he would be able to see around him. There was no one about, so, stripping down to his underwear, he took a deep breath and dived in. It was icy cold, and there was a strong current. But he was fit, and he was determined.

Down, down he went for about twenty feet. His eyes, closed during the dive, were now open. To his relief the water around him was relatively clean and clear. He was able to see the bottom without too much difficulty.

It took six dives, with him holding his breath each time for as long as he could, before he found what he was seeking. The spade was there on the bottom, wedged between two rocks! He dragged it up the bank, holding it carefully to avoid spoiling any fingerprints that might be on it, tied it to the motorcycle, and set off home.

The Chameleon Candidate

Next day, another slice of luck came his way. He discovered that his grocery round included the canteen of a science laboratory. This gave him the idea of making friends with one of the young technicians. He put on the charm and soon was able to ask for a favor, the extraction of fingerprints from the camera and the spade! Within a week he got his prints.

The next part of the plan was more difficult, to get Bundy's own prints to see if they matched. He wracked his brains. He mustn't fail now. Then he recalled overhearing Bundy once boast that he had been an officer in the National Guard in his youth. Surely fingerprints would be taken for administration purposes?

His luck held. The headquarters of the Alabama National Guard were in Montgomery and again his new job came to his rescue. As well as groceries, his firm had a contract to supply cigarettes and pipe tobacco to these headquarters. Now he was armed with the perfect excuse to enter the building.

Quickly, he worked on his next contact, a pretty girl named Janie, who worked as a clerk in the filing section. Flirting with her, he soon felt secure enough to beg a favor. Could he see Lieutenant Bundy's file? The request was met with a blank stare. He was ready with the follow-up. Cyrus Bundy was his stepfather. He had given permission for access to his file. It was all part of some family research he was currently engaged in, and he needed to check a number of facts.

He hoped she wouldn't insist on having Bundy's authority in writing, but she did. It was more than her job was worth if she bent the rules, even for him! Julius had anticipated this, however. During the days at the ranch when he was bored and with nothing to do, he'd practiced forging Bundy's signature to the stage where he had perfected it. He had felt it might come in useful sometime. That time had come. Next day he returned with a hand written note, forged in Bundy's writing, complete with signature, giving the bearer permission to look at his file.

After checking the signature with the ones in the file, Janie was

Nine

satisfied. Julius got access to the file and a powerful photocopier to allow him to magnify the fingerprints.

Back at the hostel, he studied these against the ones from the camera and the spade. As far as he could tell, the prints matched perfectly.

The next problem was to get someone in authority to listen to his story. He desperately needed someone to take him seriously. Over the next few days he spoke with several police officers. He even went to the District Attorney's office. Nobody wanted to know! Each person in turn dismissed him out of hand. They told him not only was he wasting his time, but also theirs. The case was closed and could not be re-opened on the strength of what he had told them. Julius was barely able to control his frustration. Finally, he asked to see the Sheriff. The request was denied.

When he was at the police station a young sergeant, more pleasant than the rest, took him aside and explained that even if he did succeed in having the case re-opened, the verdict would be the same. No Alabama court would ever bring a conviction against Bundy. He was too big, too powerful – too useful. He even hinted that Bundy had the Sheriff in his pocket.

Suddenly, as the sergeant was speaking, what had to be done entered Julius's mind. He must kill Bundy himself. Despite all his efforts, he now knew this was the only way for someone like him, a nobody with a police record, to get justice.

That Sunday, Julius went to his mother's grave in the Municipal Cemetery and said a prayer. He told her he was going to get revenge for her murder soon.

'Bundy'll pay fer this Ma, ah promise yah!' Tears were streaming down his face.

During the next few frustrating days, Julius's thoughts turned more than once to his goody two shoes brother. He wondered what he was doing in New York. He was bound to be a big shot by now. He had no way of knowing he was a lawyer, he'd left the ranch before Selina had a chance to tell him.

The Chameleon Candidate

But Nathan was of no use to him now. Even if his pride had allowed him to seek his brother's help, he had no contact address. He would have to do this alone and unaided. If he didn't do it now, Bundy would get away with it forever. That must not be allowed to happen. Now that he had made up his mind there would be no turning back. He was quite clear-headed and totally cold-blooded about what he was going to do. As far as he was concerned, he was carrying out the most natural act in the world. If the proper authorities were not prepared to dispense justice, then he must. As for him, if he got away with it, that would be well and good. He would genuinely try to make a new life for himself. Perhaps he would even return to Mississippi? If he didn't get away with it, then he would do time, a lot of time. Perhaps he would even get the chair? One way or the other, he was not too concerned.

It was now Wednesday. Julius would aim to carry out the execution that Friday night. He would return to the ranch, hoping not to be seen, prepare a suitable weapon and await his victim. The whole operation had organized itself neatly in his mind now. He didn't have to say anything to anybody any more. No more explanations, rejections or humiliations. He would do a clean job, and then get the hell out of Montgomery forever.

At dusk on the Friday, Julius hitched a lift to the ranch. He slipped through the ornate black and gold wrought iron gates, adorned with two jet-black mustangs. He made his way up the driveway, using cover provided by the trees. He knew the rear door would probably be unlocked.

His luck held. He tiptoed through the rear hall. As he passed the kitchen he noted a light shining under the closed door. He entered the dining room and made for the gun cabinet. He selected a pearl handled Colt 45, filling the chamber with six bullets. He was not interested in playing Russian roulette with Bundy. He knew that this gun was one half of a matched pair, the other Bundy kept in a drawer by his bed. The clock in the hall said a quarter after nine. He resigned himself to several hours' wait.

Nine

Waiting was of no consequence. He had a job to do. If for some reason it wasn't done that night, then he would do it the following one. He went into the room that once was his bedroom. It was a good room to use for his operational headquarters, the windows allowed a clear view over the driveway. He had every reason to believe that no one knew he was in the house.

A few minutes after midnight, Julius watched as the reflection of Bundy's headlights silhouetted the trees as the Pontiac swung in from the highway. He stiffened in the darkness.

Bundy scrunched to a halt at the front door. He staggered out of the car, almost measuring his length on the ground. Obviously a considerable amount of booze had been consumed. Julius wasn't sure whether that was a good or a bad thing in the light of what was going to happen. A crash in the hall. Oaths. Bundy's raised voice. Finally he made it to the landing, Julius could hear him staggering towards his bedroom.

He waited a few minutes, then crossed the corridor. Bundy's door was open; he was seated at the side of the bed, his ten-gallon hat at a crazy angle on his head.

Hearing a noise, Bundy turned. Slowly, recognition dawned.

'What the... not yah agin. Git outa here, yah damn little fucker. I have no business with yeh!'

'Oh, but yah has Cyrus, fer ah sure enough has business with you!' Julius was ice cool as he closed and locked the door behind him. By this point, Bundy smelled a rat. He reached for the gun in his drawer.

Julius was prepared. It made him feel better that his opponent was armed. Rock steady, he pointed his weapon straight at Bundy's heart.

Bundy raised his gun, but was having great difficulty in keeping it still.

'Whaddya mean, yah has business with me?'
'Yah knows very well.'
'Whaddya talkin' about?'

'Justice. That's what ah'm talkin' about.'

For a moment Bundy gazed about him blankly. Then a crafty look took over his face.

'Yah murdered mah Ma, gunned her down in cold blood, yah fuckin' swine!' Julius was unable to keep the emotion out of his voice.

'So what, she was a nosy slut. She deserved it!'

Julius could hardly believe what he was hearing. 'Yah admits it then?'

In response, Bundy pulled the trigger. The bullet grazed Julius's shoulder, embedding itself in the wall behind him.

'Ah'm awful glad yah done that, Cyrus. Now ah kin plead self-defense!'

A scared look crossed Bundy's face. 'Yah wouldn't dare!'

Julius pulled the trigger, firing one no nonsense shot straight for the heart. Momentarily Bundy, who hadn't stood up in all this time, looked dazed. Then, in slow motion, he toppled sideways, crashing onto the floor with a thump and lay still.

Moments later, there was a furious hammering at the door. Now was the time for Julius's escape plan. Pocketing the gun, he leapt over Bundy's prostrate body to the window beyond. He flung it open. He knew there was a drainpipe close by that led to the ground. He felt for it and slid down just as he heard the door being smashed in. He dropped the final ten feet to the ground and ran for Bundy's car. As he suspected, the keys were in the ignition. He started the engine and took off at high speed down the driveway, sweeping out in triumph onto the highway.

Chapter Ten

When Julius fled the ranch that night, he was convinced that Cyrus Bundy had died instantly. He knew his aim was true, and he had seen the bullet enter the chest. By all logic, Bundy should have died there and then.

Unfortunately for Julius, this was not the case. The bullet had indeed been fired into the general area of the heart, missing the heart muscle by a fraction of an inch. But it did destroy the aorta, the main heart artery. As a result, Bundy did not die instantly. He had time to gasp out Julius's name to Freestone before he expired.

This put a very different complexion on the whole business. It was something Julius had no way of knowing, as he sped off into the darkness back to the hostel, enjoying a totally false sense of security. He was certain none of the servants even knew he was there, so how could anyone possibly link him with the crime?

He knew Bundy's car would soon be reported missing. Almost new, it would be worth a great deal of money. So much so that Julius was tempted to consider selling it, or even keeping it. But he was intelligent enough to realize either action would be fraught with danger. For the present he would park the vehicle at the end of the street, and in the morning find a suitable place to abandon it. As it was, he was emotionally exhausted and badly in need of sleep. Tomorrow could look after itself

At eight o'clock in the morning someone knocked on his door. It was the hostel warden accompanied by two policemen. He got out of bed. Startled, he stood to face them. They are quick off the mark, he thought, but still he wasn't unduly concerned. He was expecting it to be something to do with the car. He cursed himself for his laziness in not dealing with it before he went to bed. He did wonder, however, how the police had made the connection with him, and so quickly. He assumed someone must have seen him in the car.

The warden left. One of the policemen said, 'Julius Beauregarde?'

'Yeah.'

'We are arresting you for the murder of your stepfather, Cyrus Bundy. You do not have to say anything...'

His rights were read.

Julius couldn't believe what he was hearing. All sorts of wild thoughts chased through his mind. What had gone wrong? Had he been seen, and by whom? He found himself incapable of speech.

The policemen waited while he dressed, then slipped handcuffs on him. He was led out to a waiting police car. On the journey to the station, he tried asking questions, but got no response. Then, for the second time in his short life, he was thrown into a cell. All that long day he lay on his bunk staring at the ceiling. No one came near him.

At daylight the following morning, he was shaken awake by a guard with his breakfast.

'What the hell am ah doin' here?' he said.

'If ah were you boy, ah'd git me a lawyer,' the man said.

'Ah've no money fer lawyers!'

'That's yer problem boy!' The guard went out, locking the door.

Later that day, by means of putting his face hard against the bars, Julius discovered he could just see down the corridor. He saw the young sergeant who'd been friendly to him before, speaking to someone. He called out. The sergeant came down. He told him his problem.

'Leave it to me, son,' the sergeant said.

Next morning a nondescript little man with a hooked nose and an enormous beard was shown into his cell. He introduced himself as Jacob Finklestein. He was the lawyer sent to represent Julius.

Julius explained he had no money. The little man beamed and

Ten

spread his hands, 'I am a legal aid lawyer, young man. The state will pay my fees.'

In the course of the conversation with Finklestein, Julius was to learn that Bundy had not died instantly, as he had thought. He had survived long enough to gasp out Julius's name. The lawyer pointed out that this revelation from a dying man would be accepted in court as a dying declaration.

The police had made a positive connection between Bundy's Pontiac and Julius. His fingerprints were on the steering wheel. They'd matched them with the ones in his police file. It was a tough case to answer. It only remained to see how successful Finklestein would be in having the charges reduced to manslaughter.

'You'd better level with me, young man. First-degree murder holds the death penalty!' Finklestein warned.

Despite his earlier laid back attitude, Julius was now scared, and felt very alone. He told his side of the story, leaving nothing out, explaining that he had actual proof Bundy had murdered his mother.

Within ten days, Finklestein had prepared his case. This was a mixture of information Julius had fed him, together with positive legal points, all dressed up in a clever package that only a lawyer with his experience could sell with any chance of success. He had already managed to have the charge reduced to justifiable homicide. But the fact that Julius had come armed with intent to kill his stepfather, weighed heavily against him.

Against Finklestein's advice, Julius himself insisted that this fact be stated. He wanted the whole world to know that this was the only way in which he felt that he could obtain justice.

At the end of the trial, the jury was out for less than an hour. The verdict was unanimous – guilty. Judge Virgil Lawson, his shock of white hair sticking from his head as if he'd been sent to the chair himself, pronounced sentence in slow measured tones.

'Twelve years in the Alabama State Penitentiary!'

A gasp echoed around the courtroom. Given all the evidence in the defendant's favor, this was a harsh sentence indeed for one so young, with only a previous drug offence on his record.

Without a backward glance, Julius, his face impassive, was taken down to begin his sentence.

Chapter Eleven

While all these terrible things had been happening in Alabama, Nathan, in New York, was blissfully ignorant of all of them. He had no way of knowing that his mother was dead, murdered by her husband, or that his brother had been sentenced to twelve years in prison for Bundy's murder. Nathan had never met his stepfather, but he knew from the tone of Selina's letters that he was not a nice man. Nathan was now twenty-six, had been a qualified lawyer for several years, and was making great strides in his law practice.

In the middle of his first administration, Richard Nixon was struggling to bring the war in Vietnam to a close. This monster of a war had been more costly and much more damaging to the American economy than anyone could have predicted. By the end of that summer, inflation had become so rampant that Nixon was forced to reverse his domestic policy overnight. Over three years had passed without major urban riots. This was good, in that the riots themselves were over, but unfortunately the conditions that were supposed to have produced them in the first place were little changed. Indeed, in certain aspects they were worse. In August, pressure on the dollar became so great that it had to be devalued for the first time in forty years.

Nathan was still greatly fired with ambition. He knew he possessed the necessary, albeit quiet, drive to get on. Extremely able, he had a first class brain. But he still lacked the cunning and street fighting instincts of his brother.

While he was happy to work as part of a team, he never showed any great competitive streak, not even at college, in what was a highly competitive forum. He was content to plough his own lonely furrow.

By now he had taken shape as a highly competent and interesting individual. Tall, dark and forever courteous, with a touch of old fashioned Southern charm, he was kind and patient with everybody, and so strikingly handsome that when he walked into a room, heads would turn – especially female ones.

He gave the impression, which was accurate, that he was genuinely unaware of his good looks. Unlike most other young men of his age, who, for the most part had less going for them, he was reserved, not at all keen to 'strut his stuff'.

Nathan was a complicated person. The truth was he lacked confidence, even the inner self-assurance that would have allowed him to flirt, like many young men did, flitting like a butterfly from girl to girl. He was far too serious for any of that.

By the end of the year he was seeing a girl on a regular basis. Janet Pulitzer, slim, dark and easy on the eye, was from Idaho. She had been an active Civil Rights worker and was now employed in his office.

Janet was soon to discover, however, that Nathan was not ready to make the serious commitment to her that she craved. He had things to do, he had to make money. But more importantly, he needed to further his political ambitions without being distracted by serious affairs of the heart. In truth, the girl did have a certain attraction for him. She was pleasant looking rather than beautiful, with an open humorous face. She also had a very graceful style of moving, giving the impression that she was walking permanently on her tip toes, as is done in Irish dancing. Nathan prided himself that he could always tell if a girl was a good dancer just by the way in which she moved.

Janet was a good dancer and loved to dance. There were many times when she wished for nothing more than that she and Nathan could dance the night away.

In many ways she reminded Nathan of what he remembered of his mother. Selina had those dark attractive looks, coupled with a graceful way of moving. After all, Selina had had to be a good

Eleven

dancer, in those days her livelihood depended on it!

Ever since his first day in New York, when Aunt Nessie had pointed out Central Park to him, Nathan had developed a never-ending fascination for the place. He marveled at this huge self contained forest park set right in the center of the busiest metropolis in the world.

Often he would walk there from his office, a ten-minute stroll, to have a picnic lunch. Summer evenings would find him there, sitting on a bench, or ambling in the cool shade of the trees. It was a ready-made haven for busy people such as he, those who enjoyed their own company. This was especially true for people who were brought up in a rural state, finding themselves in New York without even the color of a window box.

Those who saw Nathan in the Park could never have guessed that his childhood had been so deprived, both emotionally and financially. Or, with his good looks, smart clothes, erect bearing and educated speech with just a touch of Southern drawl, that he had been one of thousands of poor white trash Mississippi kids.

Yet again, perceptive folk, who might have had occasion to tune in for tell tale signs, could see ambition quietly oozing out of Nathan Beauregarde. They would wonder what had given him this undoubted resolve. They might guess it was this same deprived childhood that had been the tinderbox that lit his flame, crystallizing him into the man he had undoubtedly become.

Nathan would use his time spent in the Park as a sounding board for human behavior. He would do a great deal of thinking and planning there. The rich and divergent tapestry of behavior it offered up constantly fascinated him.

One day he was struck by the ugliness of two women. One in particular, perhaps the elder, had such a bony, hideous face that he was convinced she must have been wearing a mask. Several times he had to resist the ridiculous temptation to rush forward to tear off the mask, revealing perhaps a fairy princess!

Her companion was ugly too, there was no mistake about it. But to Nathan's eyes, she possessed a gentler kind of ugliness, an ugliness that was more bearable to the onlooker. An ugliness that said it wasn't really an unkind twist of nature, especially when it was broken up with a smile that lit up her whole face.

Another fascination for Nathan in his beloved Park was one particular tree. It was a huge silvery colored solitary tree standing at well over a hundred feet high. It never grew any foliage on it. Even in the height of summer, when all around was a bright verdant green, or after a rainstorm, not a leaf or bud could be seen on it.

Nathan convinced himself that the tree must either be dead, or man made. But who would make such a tree and put it in such a place, and for what purpose? One day his curiosity got the better of him. He took a penknife from his pocket and cut deeply into the bark. The wood was hard and unresponsive to the sharp blade of the knife. He cut off a section of the wood to examine it, and then carved his initials beside it. This told him the tree was neither manmade nor dead. If it had been dead the sheer weight would have toppled it over a long time ago. This was a minor mystery in his life destined never to be solved!

If Mayo Cleveland had a fault, and in Nathan's eyes he didn't, it would have been that he was a little too touchy at times for his own good. When he was in a certain mood, he appeared to feel he had the monopoly on making sarcastic remarks just for the sake of it. His students had noticed it. These same students had also noticed that he wasn't able to take as good as he handed out. He had a low threshold for personal criticism.

Within the year, Cleveland was running for nomination for the Senate, standing as an Independent for New York State, given that his family originated in Albany. He had managed, with Nathan's help, to build up a fine campaign team. Their work had helped him already to his position as a Councilor. Now he was confident the same team would further propel him up the ladder towards Washington and the Senate.

If he could achieve Senator status, then he would be in a good

Eleven

position to concentrate on his ultimate ambition – the Presidency. He made no secret of this. Knowing this ambition of old, and looking now at his handsome, well-bred face and oh so determined jaw, Nathan, for one, was totally convinced, barring accidents, that Mayo Cleveland would achieve his aim.

Nathan was still seeing Janet more or less regularly, but despite this his feelings for her were never anything more than superficial. He had not gone to bed with her, and had no plans to do so. He was old-fashioned enough to believe that you do not bed your woman before the wedding night.

Increasingly, he was becoming more determined not to be hurried into the most important decision any man can make, that of choosing a wife.

He was making steady, if not spectacular, money in the law practice in which he was now a junior partner. He was gaining a reputation as a people's lawyer, one who was prepared to take on small cases just as readily as the bigger ones.

There were times when things were going really well that Nathan would dream of running for President himself. But in his more worldly moments he knew rarely was that a possibility for run of the mill junior lawyers, no matter what their ability.

There had to be another dimension for this to happen. Luck certainly, and timing, but something else was needed too. There had to be an enormous well of self-confidence deep inside a person, linked to push, stamina, tolerance and the ability to shake off disappointment. He didn't feel that he had any of these qualities in sufficient measure, but he did recognize them in Mayo Cleveland.

Cleveland, like himself, was delaying settling down, even though he knew it would help his political ambitions to have a wife.

One spring day he bought himself a new car, a huge, powerful, bright red Ford Thunderbird sports car. He had always liked to drive fast, as he liked to do everything at speed. Now he chose to drive even faster. It gave him a real feeling of power and control, he claimed.

Soon he was subjecting Nathan, a far more cautious character with little ambition for speed, to hair-raising drives, thundering down the back roads of his native New York State at well over a hundred miles per hour.

One Sunday in the fall, Mayo Cleveland invited Nathan to spend the day at his country club near Newburgh on the Hudson River, close to where it wound around the rocky hills surrounding West Point. Nathan, who knew Cleveland was not in the habit of inviting work colleagues to his club, was flattered and greatly looking forward to the experience. He had never been to a country club before, and he knew this to be a prestigious one.

The day was beautiful and the russet foliage surrounding the clubhouse was quite spectacular in the sunshine. For his part, Cleveland spent the greater part of the day within arms reach of the bar, cultivating the wealthy and powerful members, airing his ideas and ambitions to all who would listen. Always on a vote catching exercise, Nathan thought wryly. Cleveland was in his element and on his very best form that day, playing King holding court to a captive audience. People of substance were listening to him, asking him questions and generally giving him the respect his temperament craved.

By the middle of the afternoon, Nathan began to feel a small cold frog jump into his heart as he couldn't help but note the number of times his host's glass was replenished. Later that evening, as they left for home, Nathan felt compelled to offer to drive. He knew before he spoke his offer would be rejected. Under no circumstances would Cleveland let anyone else drive his precious Thunderbird.

'Of course I'm OK, old friend,' he said. 'You worry too much. I can handle my drink!' The slurring of his words gave the lie to that statement.

In silence, they set off at high speed for the city. The frog in Nathan's heart was disinclined to go away.

Halfway home, just as it was getting dusk, while they were still in

Eleven

the countryside, Cleveland rounded a bend in the road that should have been negotiated at less than fifty at over a hundred miles per hour. In the middle distance a huge tractor with trailer began to chug out of a side road, effectively blocking off two thirds of the road. Cleveland's last minute desperate attempts to avoid a collision were too late and to no avail. Nothing could save them. During the final terrifying seconds before the inevitable crash, Nathan closed his eyes...

One week later he awoke in a bed in Bellevue Hospital. He was covered from head to toe with bruises, and had suffered a fractured skull as a result of his head hitting the windshield. Miraculously, other than that he was unhurt.

Something inside him made him hesitate about inquiring as to the fate of his friend. When he did get around to it, he was informed that Mayo Cleveland had died instantly in the crash. Once the reality had sunk in, Nathan couldn't help feeling that his meaningful life was also over.

He recovered quickly enough, physically at any rate, but it took a long time before his mental scars healed.

Shortly after emerging from the coma, Nathan was discharged from hospital, only to discover that his friend had already been buried in the family grave in Albany.

Looking back, Nathan often wondered whether Mayo Cleveland had some sort of premonition about his early death. Some folk do. There was no doubt that he worked and pushed and studied and negotiated as if he knew his time on earth was limited. The maximum achievement had to be garnered into the limited span of his days.

Chapter Twelve

A whole year later Nathan was still struggling with his feelings of loss in the aftermath of the death of his friend, Mayo Cleveland. He decided that something would have to be done about his love life. Janet was still his girl, but he felt now he was not only wasting her time, but also his own.

He must end the relationship. She was a good worker, so he couldn't sack her. He blamed himself for displaying an interest during the early days of their relationship. Office relationships rarely worked, he should have known that. He also knew there was nothing quite so painful for a pretty girl as a bout of unrequited love.

Greatly to his relief, the situation resolved itself. One day she presented him with a set of figures that were inaccurate, something unheard of in her work before. Nathan felt he was entitled to rebuke her. Janet burst into floods of tears and ran from the room. Next morning her resignation was on his desk. He was quick to accept it. In turn he gave her a glowing reference, one that would help her to find another position.

In private, he breathed a huge sigh of relief. He had not wanted to hurt her, but he knew he was not the man for her. He consoled himself, therefore, with the thought that he was doing both of them a favor. Life went on. Soon it was the beginning of a new year. Now Nathan began to pull out all stops to seek a nomination to the Senate himself. Like his hero Cleveland, he would run on his own Independent ticket, aiming to become a Senator as Cleveland had hoped to be at the time of his death. Politics, and the hope of high political office, had now taken over his life. Nothing else seemed to matter. He had, in effect, become the man of destiny that Mayo

Twelve

Cleveland had once been. Even as a small boy back in Mississippi, he knew he was destined for something important, but had no idea what it was. Now he knew – he would run for The Presidency!

Having no domestic life worth talking about, he could devote a great deal of time towards working for that ambition. Inside himself he had the firm conviction that God was wanting him to carry on where his friend had been forced to leave off.

Always a firm believer in the Almighty, Nathan still said his prayers every night in the way he'd been taught all those years ago, not by Selina, but by Reverend Sam McColgan. If the old man was still alive, he would have been pleased with him. He would have discovered he had managed to instill in the boy a deep religious faith, a faith he would never lose.

Since he had first arrived in New York, Nathan had attended Grace Catholic Church with Aunt Nessie. He really attended more to please the old lady than for any other reason. But it had given him the discipline of regular church attendance, something that he was beginning to miss. Now, since Aunt Nessie's death, Nathan felt no desire to continue in the Catholic faith. He began to experience a great need to get back to his own Baptist tradition.

In the wake of Janet Pulitzer leaving, Nathan took the opportunity to up-grade her post. He now advertised for a private secretary. He interviewed a number of applicants until he found one that suited him.

Miranda Van Dusberg came to him with immaculate references. She was from Connecticut. Her parents' home was next door to the house once owned by Mark Twain, from where he wrote many of his best sellers.

In her early twenties, poised and attractive rather than beautiful, she was half Dutch and half German. She had class written all over her. What appealed to Nathan most of all was the genuine warmth of her manner. With absolutely nothing to prove, she treated all his clients in the same friendly way, be they from the Bronx, Queens or affluent Manhattan. She had a gift of looking each person directly in the eye, giving the impression they had been singled out for special treatment that day. When she smiled her whole face lit up like one of heaven's angels.

By the time his thirty-third birthday came along in April, Nathan had put together his new campaign team. He was fortunate in being able to use people who had worked for Mayo Cleveland

He chose Newt Ludlow as his manager. Ludlow had been on the election circuit for years, and had been Cleveland's manager. He knew all the pit-falls and tricks of the trade. In his late fifties, Ludlow was sound rather than inspired, with a solid reassuring face. He was an administrator and adviser rather than a leader. Leadership was up to Nathan. He needed to provide as much magic and panache as possible, in order to drive his little team forward to the success he so desperately wanted.

In many respects, Nathan's independent policies mirrored those of Cleveland, but there were certain differences. For example, Cleveland had been keen to implement most aspects of the Civil Rights program. In doing this he had tended to lack the in-depth knowledge of how colored folk thought. This was something Nathan had in full measure, which was understandable; Cleveland was an intellectual from the North, while Nathan had grown up with coloreds in Mississippi.

Whites who had experienced this normally found themselves in one of two camps. The majority felt deep hatred and mistrust, wanting only to '...keep the nigger in his place...', the others feeling complete empathy with their colored neighbors, genuinely wanting to stretch out the hand of friendship to them.

But what was even more striking was the utter dissimilarity in style and approach between the two men. Where Cleveland had been over-confident, Nathan was ultra cautious. Where Cleveland had been charming but vacillating, Nathan, once he made up his mind, was steady and assured. Where Cleveland had wheedled and occasionally hectored in order to get his point across, Nathan was quiet and reassuring, never raising his voice. Cleveland, in his

Twelve

stride, with the flow going and facing a receptive audience, could sometimes labor matters to the point of boredom. Nathan never did this, having a built in horror of boring people.

Nathan was sufficiently astute and self-analytical to realize that he lacked the showmanship and magic of delivery that Cleveland, for the most part, had possessed. This he would never have, it was something one is either born with or not. Tactics could be worked on, delivery of speeches improved, but if the natural extroverted fire in the belly is absent, there is little that can be done about it, except to highlight and hone the positive talents that he did have.

He was still tortured by shyness, a considerable lack of confidence, something he'd fought all his life to overcome. As the years rolled on and he became more mature and knowledgeable, he also became adept at masking this from the world – at least for most of the time.

Nathan also prided himself in always doing his homework. Whether it was in writing speeches or researching some subject, he was always meticulous, leaving nothing to chance. Cleveland had rarely done any more than the minimum of research, relying on his charm and ability to manufacture acceptable off the cuff answers to see him through. He had been a past master in creating a smoke screen around the matter in hand. If he wasn't sure of his ground, he sometimes resorted to complete inaccuracies, if not downright lies. But all this was done with such skill and verve that the clients usually went away well satisfied.

When Nathan was first qualified, he spent countless hours burning the midnight oil, working on briefs, polishing and honing his presentations to the court. He was to adapt these same disciplines to his political career.

Ironically, even before Mayo Cleveland's untimely death, a slow but sure seed had been germinating in Nathan's soul, a seed of political ambition. Now that seed had sprouted inside him, destined to propel him forward.

So it was that now a determination grew in Nathan to pick up

Mayo Cleveland's political standard from where it had lain at the scene of the horrific car crash on the highway between Albany and New York City, at the spot where his very life had been jolted from its frame. He felt his mission was to seize this Standard, raise it high, hold it tight, ever so tight, and begin the long, perhaps impossible, climb up Capitol Hill and ultimately into the White House.

In effect, Nathan Beauregarde was stepping into Mayo Cleveland's shoes.

Chapter Thirteen

It was during one of these preparation sessions in the 42nd Street Library, a library with a research department containing back copies of all American newspapers, that Nathan was to discover the dreadful truth about his family in Alabama.

One afternoon, he was leafing through the files, following up on issues dear to his heart, matters a Senator in the making should know about, when his eye caught a headline in an Alabama newspaper, The Montgomery Herald.

The headline read: 'Rancher's Wife Murdered'. He read on, his heart doing a war dance in his chest. He had to peruse several issues before he managed to get to grips with the whole terrible business. He read of the discovery of Selina's body ten miles from the scene of the execution of the Negro Tandy. '...all the hallmarks of a Ku Klux Klan execution...,' the paper said.

He read on with mounting horror. In both cases a bland verdict, not reflecting the seriousness of the crimes, had been brought in. Then he read of the murder of Cyrus Bundy, his own stepfather. Finally he read that his twin brother, Julius, had been arrested and convicted of the manslaughter of Bundy, and had been sentenced to twelve years in Alabama State Prison.

He read the background information, gleaned by the paper, as to his brother's life style, leading up to the death of Bundy. He read about his years of being a hippy, a drug user, a pusher and a general down and out.

Within one dreadful hour, the worst hour of his life, Nathan had been exposed to all the terrible and totally unexpected news pertaining to the fate of his entire family.

In a daze, he staggered out of the library and sank onto a bench

The Chameleon Candidate

in Bryant Park. He was in an agony of mental turmoil. Surely something was wrong? It must be some dreadful hoax; the papers must have got it wrong. His emotions had yet to kick in.

Finally, slowly, he fought to rationalize the news. It was so terrible that he couldn't allow his mind to take all of it in at once. Instead, he had to sift it in piece by piece.

Despite the fact that he'd never met Bundy, he had managed to acquire some insight into the man's character through Selina's infrequent letters. He knew that all had not been well. Latterly, she had opened up with him, telling him of her unhappiness with Bundy.

Hour after hour passed as he sat transfixed to the bench, until the streetlights came on around the park. Desperately, he fought to keep his mind from panicking, to keep it in gear, and in some shape to reason through this nightmare.

Some instinct told him it was Bundy who murdered their mother. He assumed Julius had thought so too, and had done for him. Once he did get his lawyer's analytical mind under control, it went back and back again to the newspaper's comments about the Ku Klux Klan. The more he thought about it, the more convinced he was becoming that Bundy had been involved with the Klan. From Selina's description of him, it would seem he was just the type of white intolerant racist who would be. If Selina had discovered this, and he had found out, she could well have signed her own death warrant.

Next morning, after a sleepless night, Nathan put through a call to the Montgomery police. They confirmed all he had read. He asked for an interview with the Sheriff for the afternoon of the following day. He booked a flight to Montgomery, leaving his office work in the capable hands of Miranda Van Dusberg. He told her he was going south on business, and would be back before the end of the week.

On the plane, his mind was still in turmoil, but by now emotion had begun to creep in. His feelings had crystallized into a disturb-

Thirteen

ing mixture of guilt and resentment. He felt deep resentment about the scale of his early domestic deprivation. He resented the fact that he should now be able to bask in the success he had found in New York, but because of what he had recently learnt, all the old guilt had flooded back into his system, effectively nullifying any feelings of well being he had begun to build up.

Looking back, he wondered why he had not known about the dreadful series of happenings in Alabama long before he did. For sure, they had not found their way into any of the New York papers. He could only assume that, horrendous as they undoubtedly were in Alabama, with so much else going on in the country the size of America, they just didn't warrant a mention in New York.

Even though Selina's letters to him had become increasingly intermittent, with an element of wildness about them, when they ceased altogether he felt he should have known that something was very wrong.

All in all, he was very uncertain as to how to handle matters when he did reach Alabama. For the present he had ruled out making contact with Idle Winds, Mississippi. Apart from the letters he'd received from Reverend Sam McColgan written in response to his, he had not heard from anyone there and, so far as he knew, his mother had severed all connections.

This train of thought set him thinking about his brother Julius. The good looking, rebellious, at times downright unpleasant little boy, capable of mean and vicious acts, whom he hadn't seen for over twenty years. He recalled the feelings of resentment that, even then, he felt Julius had for him. By now these could have turned into an obsession. He hoped not.

The flight took a little over two hours, but to Nathan it seemed a lifetime. Now nothing could lift the black dog blanket of doom filled depression and hopelessness that had descended about his shoulders.

He had always been subject to fits of nervous depression; these would attack him from time to time. This, however, was a serious low. Nothing could lift it, not even a pretty airhostess offering him a drink, or the sun streaming through the windows of the huge silver bird as it roared its way southward.

At the airport Nathan took a taxi to the center of Montgomery, a journey of about fifteen minutes. There he booked into a small, comfortable two star hotel.

It was midday. He had a drink at the hotel bar, a light lunch, and then set off for the police station.

Jed Hathaway was the Montgomery police chief. Before he left New York, and through his legal contacts, Nathan discovered that Hathaway had earned himself something of a dubious reputation. Suspicion about a number of matters surrounding him over the years had remained. But there had never seemed to be sufficient evidence to make charges against him, or no one around with sufficient balls to make them! He was too well entrenched with the local political heavyweights for his position ever to have been in serious jeopardy.

In the event, Nathan took an instant dislike to him, and felt it was reciprocated. Hathaway possessed an unctuous and insincere manner. He had the flat, dull yet dangerous eyes of a snake. Even his voice was low and peppered with sibilant hisses. Into the bargain he had the worst set of false teeth Nathan had ever seen gracing anyone's mouth.

There was something about badly fitting false teeth that had always irritated the immaculate Nathan. During the years he practiced as a lawyer, he had noticed many people in high places who had their appearance spoiled by poorly fitted false teeth.

From the start, Hathaway's attitude was one of barely concealed hostility. When Nathan began his probing, as he was perfectly entitled to do, Hathaway answered his questions in as offhand a manner as he felt he could get away with. An hour in the man's company left Nathan feeling like the intruder he was undoubtedly meant to feel. When he inquired as to why the coroner had felt the

Thirteen

need to bring in such bland verdicts on all three deaths, Nathan was met with a hostile stare and a dismissive shrug of the shoulders.

Finally, after it became obvious he was wasting his time, Nathan terminated the interview. On his way out he was issued with a special pass allowing him access to his brother.

The Alabama State Prison was situated in open country some twenty miles south west of Montgomery. A huge clinical-gray purpose-built edifice, it had been constructed some ten years previously to cater for the ever increasing number of crimes carried out in the state as a result of the drug abuse of the sixties. Practical, but featureless, it was set about with a number of fierce looking uniformed guards, handling equally fierce looking dogs. High on the walls of this fortress were four gun emplacements, one on each corner of the building, manned by guards with machine guns. These vantage points allowed the guards an unlimited bird's eye view over the plateau.

Instructing his taxi driver to wait, Nathan was conducted through several massive security gates, and then down a series of long cold corridors, each crammed with barred cells on either side. Finally they came to a halt at the end of the fourth corridor. The guard unlocked the door with a key from an enormous bunch, secured by a chain, to his belt.

He said one word to the occupant, 'Visitor!' He stepped back, hovering in the corridor. Nathan moved across the threshold of the cell. There, seated hunched on a tiny bed, was a carbon copy of himself.

Suddenly his throat was dry. It took him all his time to croak out, 'Hello, Julius!'

The figure on the bed might have been dead. It didn't speak. It didn't stand up. It didn't even look up.

Nathan walked forward proffering his hand. Only then did Julius look up. He did not take his hand.

'Don't you recognize me? It's me... Nathan!'

The Chameleon Candidate

'Ah know who yah are. But ah don't know what yah doin' here.' Julius's voice was heavy with hostility.

Nathan had prepared himself for some resentment on his brother's part, but somehow the depth and tone of this remark came as a shock.

'Julius, I've come to help you, can't you see that? Why can't we let bygones be bygones?'

'Too late fer that!' Julius stared at the ground.

'It's never too late, Julius. A lot of water has flowed under the bridge since we saw each other last. A lot of things have happened.'

'Yah kin say that agin!'

Nathan began to try to explain that he had only just read about the tragedies in a New York library. He told about the intermittent correspondence he had carried on with their mother, but that it had dried up.

He pointed out that New York was a huge place, and matters in Alabama, no matter how horrific, were not newsworthy there. He could see the look of disbelief that crossed his brother's face as he spoke. Finally, with no encouragement to continue, he spluttered to a halt.

For the first time since Nathan entered the cell, Julius properly raised his head and stared straight at him. Nathan was startled by his huge dark eyes, so like his own, but glowing with a crazy bitter light.

When Julius spoke, his tone was sullen, laced thick with resentment. Slowly, deliberately, he began to tell his brother in no uncertain terms just how he felt about him. How he'd abandoned them for the selfish, high life he'd so obviously being enjoying in New York.

As he warmed to his theme, his voice rose to a crescendo, spitting out the crudest of words, fired at his victim in staccato machine gun fashion, using foul language to embellish his points.

By the time he'd finished this tirade, Nathan had his back to the wall of the cell. He was braced, hardly able to believe that such

Thirteen

gutter venom had issued from his own brother's lips.

He knew now, beyond a shadow of a doubt, that he had come on a fruitless mission. 'I'm sorry you feel like that, brother, really I am.' His head ached with the strength of Julius' attack.

In a final attempt to retrieve something good from this tragic situation, Nathan tried to point out that they could still be a family. There was just the two of them left now. They could help each other. It wasn't too late.

As he expected, his words were wasted. Julius, quieter now, but equally hostile, pointed out that they'd never been a proper family in the first place. The facts were there for all to see. The one with the brain had selfishly escaped to New York, leaving Selina and he to their fate.

He didn't want Nathan's help now or at any other time. He hadn't been there for them when he was needed. Now it was all too late. He hoped he would never set eyes on him again. There was nothing more to be said.

Nathan opened his mouth to say he hadn't been offered a choice about being sent away in the first place, but closed it again. What was the point? Julius knew all that as well as he did. In his present frame of mind, he would not be interested in listening.

As if in dismissal, Julius stood up, walked to the window of the cell and stared out. In response, Nathan lifted his briefcase, signaled to the guard, and walked out of the cell and the prison.

Despite himself, once he was in the safety of the rear of the taxi, something gave way inside him. Tears silently rolled down his cheeks, as he turned away for fear that the driver would see his weakness.

'God, oh God, what a mess of a family!' he said to himself.

Later that day he flew back to New York, guilt ridden, disillusioned, deeply unhappy as to the turn of events in his family. Yet, if he were truthful, not entirely surprised.

Now he knew inside himself that there was no further point in ever trying to communicate with his brother again. Julius had made that painfully clear. But he had had to make that trip. He had needed to find out what way the land lay. But God, how it hurt!

Inside himself he knew that the best and only way in which he could avenge Selina's death and try to make amends for the rotten life she'd been forced to live, was to make a big success of his own life.

Chapter Fourteen

The darkness of the day did a good job in mirroring Nathan's somber mood as he sat pensive in the rear of the jet winging its way back to New York.

He took a newspaper from the stewardess and tried his level best to concentrate on it. Despite the fact that it was full of news that normally would have interested him, he might as well have been gazing at a blank page.

He was well aware that his family structure could hardly have been considered normal, by any yardstick. But to have his mother murdered by his step-father, a man he had never seen (for he was convinced that was what had happened), then to have his twin brother imprisoned for killing Bundy, without himself knowing anything about it, beggared belief. It was the stuff nightmares were made of, and nothing in his life could ever have prepared him for it.

But what gnawed at him most of all was the devastating fact that his whole family had effectively self-destructed.

What terrible things had gone wrong? Dear God what a dreadful mess. What could he have done to avert it? Agonizing thoughts poured relentlessly through his mind. He knew now that he would be in the grip of a guilt trip till the day he died.

Back in New York he threw himself into a frenzy of work in a vain attempt to blot out the horrors of Alabama. As the months went by, he found himself no more capable of opening up about it than on the day he read about it in the library.

It was bearable during the day, just, because he ensured his work preoccupied him. It was at night, alone in the apartment, that the devils unleashed themselves, threatening to overwhelm him. It

The Chameleon Candidate

had been Julius' attitude that had been the last straw.

Unable to eat properly, daily he was filled with nervous tensions that drive away appetite. What he needed badly, and soon, was a piece of really wholesome news, something designed to lift his shattered morale. He needed a real confidence booster, some indicator that would allow him to know he wasn't really the abject failure he felt himself to be. A more hard-boiled and less compassionate person would, after the initial shock had passed, have shaken the whole matter off on the basis that they had no control over events in their early life. Consequently, they had done nothing wrong by pursuing their career in a different part of the country, while at the same time minding their own business.

But it didn't work like that with Nathan Beauregarde. His nature didn't allow him to divorce himself so easily from bearing a great deal of responsibility for such a traumatic family event.

Always something of a loner, now he was very lonely indeed – withdrawn even. He would only come out of his shell superficially during the day in order to function at all, retreating once more into it at night.

Outwardly, he still managed to retain the vestiges of his original image, that of a thrusting young lawyer, thirsty for recognition through political power. Inwardly, he was a mess, a dreadful soufflé of self-destructive negative emotions. As things stood, he was incapable of seeking solace with either male or female companions. He knew he had a massive sorting out job to do before he could offer himself as a responsible person to the electorate.

Three months after his return to New York, the news that Nathan yearned for suddenly appeared. He received a letter from the Senate Committee in Washington advising him that his status as Independent Senator for New York City had been accepted. Providing he received the necessary number of votes, a minimum of twenty-five thousand, his place in the Senate was secured.

Several months later, after grueling days and nights of electioneering, Nathan and his team counted the votes on polling day.

Fourteen

Twenty-six thousand, eight hundred people voted for the Independent Beauregarde! This success began to give him back his shattered self-confidence. The beginning of his dream was being realized.

In the main, Nathan found his work as a Senator both stimulating and satisfying. It was just what he needed. His keen legal mind helped him to cut to the root of many problems. He began to feel of value again, serving the community in a responsible capacity. Soon he found his training as a lawyer specializing in Civil Rights matters proving useful. The Mississippi man with the Northern sophistication and Southern understanding, found his voice was being listened to, not only in the Senate, but also in his constituency surgery.

He began to stand out among his peers as a man who really cared. No white man had ever stuck his neck out in a political forum so far as he had, going in to bat for the colored folk of America. They appreciated that. He understood them. He spoke their language, his speeches told them so.

In many respects he was the right man in the right place at the very right time. The whole issue of Civil Rights was still greatly to the forefront of many American minds. Even though a good deal of violent undertone had subsided, the issue was far from being satisfactorily resolved. There was much too much hard-core white supremacist thinking around to allow that.

Once Nathan had taken the decision to stand for the Senate, he made the main plank of his election campaign a referendum on Civil Rights for all Americans. He believed passionately in the rightness of this cause, and in time became extremely adept at selling it. Soon the black citizens of Harlem and the Bronx began to appreciate what he was trying to do for them, and in turn gave him their support.

Ironically, not so many years previously, Nathan would have been lynched for his forthright views on this issue, or perhaps would have been a prime target for assassination. But with the advent of enlightened leaders like Kennedy, who by the end of his administration fully supported the push for Civil Rights legislation, allied with the power and sheer charisma of Martin Luther King, as well as the considerable volume of legislation that had been passed, people were no longer able to dismiss someone with Nathan's views as an undesirable.

With this singularly new meaning to his life, once again Nathan began to burn the midnight oil preparing papers and speeches. This was important in his attempts to explain his views on the importance of gaining overall acceptance for his radical Civil Rights theories.

It was Mayo Cleveland who had first sold him the concept. Now he was embracing it, embellishing it with his own personality, theories and enthusiasm, and serving it up in as attractive a potpourri as he could, for consumption by the American voting public.

In time, he was to find he was expected to carry out a certain amount of entertaining. That was essential for a Senator. It was also common sense to pay back folk for their loyalty and to keep a finger on the pulse of New York society, to get closer to influential people to find out what they were thinking.

Now that he was earning enough money, with an allowance for staff, he was able to take clients to some of the many hotels and restaurants that abounded in the city. Membership of the Senate brought him a number of privileges, such as free office space in certain buildings, and because he represented New York City, with its huge population, he was entitled to the maximum allowance.

He became concerned about the size of his apartment. There were times when he needed to entertain at home, and it was much too small. He resolved this with the help of a realtor friend, who sold his own at a good price and found him a larger one on West 103rd Street, at the northern end of Central Park.

Yet another problem gnawed at him. It had to be resolved soon and for ever. This was the question of marriage. He had already

Fourteen

been down that road in his mind, but now that his bachelor status was being questioned in some quarters, the issue had forced its way to the front of his mind once more.

He knew he must look inside himself for one last time. Perhaps he did have latent homosexual tendencies. There were certainly those who implied it about both of them when Mayo Cleveland was alive. But if he did, he was not in the business of admitting them, even to himself. In the rare moments of self-analysis he indulged in, he had come to the conclusion he never really felt at home with women on a one-to-one basis.

Outwardly, he possessed all the qualities of a lover – good looks, poise and charm – but without any of the inclination. He did, however, appreciate the value of a woman's role in life, preferring to be surrounded by them at work. There he could admire them for the things they obviously did so much better than men.

Most of all he had an in-built horror of being humiliated, of letting people down. In consequence, he was chronically hesitant to embark on serious affairs of the heart, beginning a relationship that, perhaps, he would not be able to see through. So marriage was not for him. Not now, not ever.

He had purposely taken time to clear his mental decks for this issue. He needed an uncluttered mind in order to tackle the immense political climb he had set himself. Time spent on the marriage issue was time well spent, especially now that it had evolved into a decision. Freed emotionally for ever of such lingering thoughts, he could give all to his political career.

At about this time, he joined the congregation of Riverside Baptist Church, off Claremont Avenue.

Chapter Fifteen

It wasn't long before Nathan had been elected to a number of important Senate committees, several with strong Civil Rights connotations. Soon he was a voice to be listened to, someone with proven integrity. He was a person who was at home equally with Republicans or Democrats, yet embracing neither creed. He was fast becoming an expert on Black America. A valued speaker, he was asked to give lectures and talks to universities, colleges and at all sorts of other forums. He spoke with knowledge and compassion about the issues that mattered to him. His sincerity shone through in all his public utterances.

Nathan knew that the big reason for black under achievement, even as late as 1979, was and always had been, the fear that academic success would be taken by peer colored as a sell out to the white world, that is 'acting white'. As a result of this pathetic attitude forced on them, many gifted colored folk were not in a position to make the best of themselves, having to settle for more menial work than their qualifications and abilities had trained them for. Nathan, more than any other person in power at that time, strove to change people's attitudes, to make things easier for those blacks with talent.

One day he was gazing out of the window of his office in Lower Manhattan, thinking through the theme of a speech he was due to deliver to Congress the following day, when he noted a thick-set middle aged man and a tall slim female walking along the sidewalk.

An ordinary enough looking couple, but what struck Nathan as nice was the fact they were holding hands. They were probably husband and wife, holding hands. He liked that; it was a good sign, something that warmed his heart, and something he knew would

Fifteen

never happen to him. He was about to turn away, back to his desk, when he saw two youths emerge from an alleyway. They positioned themselves in front of the couple. Something about their movements and demeanor alerted him. Instinctively he knew what was going to happen.

He was unable to warn or help, he was too far away. Without thinking, he rushed out of his office and dashed for the elevator. As soon as it hit the ground he propelled himself out and across the street, darting in and out the traffic, regardless of his own safety. By the time he reached the sidewalk, the hoods had fled, leaving the victims on the ground.

The man sat up as Nathan approached. He was shocked and dazed, but otherwise appeared all right. The woman was a different story. Unconscious, she appeared to be having difficulty in breathing. Her pulse was weak and irregular. Nathan loosened her clothing and administered first aid.

'We've been robbed, purse stolen,' the man gasped.

Nathan looked around for help. Several people passed the scene, some actually stepping over the prone woman in their efforts to get by. Not one paused to offer assistance.

Like most people who live in New York, Nathan had become used to general crowd apathy. Nevertheless, this callousness on his own doorstep shocked him. He stepped into the road and flagged down a yellow taxicab. Using his radio, the driver called for an ambulance. It was a full ten minutes before it arrived, taking both victims to hospital. The woman still hadn't recovered consciousness. Before the ambulance spirited them away, Nathan gave the man his business card.

Several weeks later Nathan received a telephone call from Jackson, Mississippi. It was from the man he'd helped on the sidewalk. Only then did he discover his name, Toni Rossi. Rossi was a Mississippi policeman. He told Nathan how grateful he was, saying, according to the hospital, his wife Bella could have died without his help. She was now out of danger, but had sustained a fractured skull. The day of the mugging had been their wedding anniversary; they were in New York visiting Bella's sister. Rossi ended by giving Nathan his address, saying if he was ever down Mississippi way to look him up. Nathan thanked him for the call, making a mental note that he now had a grateful friend in Mississippi. Despite all, somehow he had never rejected the idea that some day he would return to his birthplace.

Predictably, as time went by, the single-minded Nathan Beauregarde grew in stature as a politician. He had come to represent for many folk a secure, identifiable, eminently sensible voice, a voice devoid of backbiting, rancor or point scoring just for the sake of it.

That year he sold his partnership in the law firm to concentrate on being a full time professional politician. This move freed up sufficient cash to allow him to underwrite future election campaigns. His courageous Independent standpoint was rapidly gaining popularity, because the timing was so right. The majority of the electorate was tired of being forced to choose between the existing old lackluster parties, both of whom had been tried, tested and found sorely lacking. It was time for a complete change, a good wholesome change; Beauregarde's Third Party could offer that!

Gradually, during that summer, Nathan began to feel a strange surge of power. For the first time ever he could see the possibility that he might just achieve his and Mayo Cleveland's dream. Up until now his mental picture had been flawed, at best hazy, sometimes not there at all. But all of a sudden it had become clear, devoid of all doubt and mist. He strove to retain that picture.

Jimmy Carter, the peanut farmer from Georgia, was limping along towards the end of his Administration, the debacle of Operation Desert Fox hanging over his head. There was little likelihood that he would get the chance of a second term. Elections were due that November.

So it was, after testing the water during those early months of the year, and taking advice from those in the know, that at the end of

Fifteen

July, Nathan Beauregarde felt strong and confident enough to put his money where his mouth was. He applied for the Presidential Nomination. He was accepted as a Third Party Candidate, running on his independent ticket. Now he really was running with the big boys.

July turned to August. Nathan and his little team began to feel that they were in with a real chance of victory. All the signs appeared to be in their favor. They fought hard to make their new Third Party a credible, desirable, sensible, political force. They jostled for a position that might just attract sufficient votes to allow them success.

Throughout the country, a vast blanket of inertia had settled over everything pertaining to politics. But millions of potential voters knew well enough they were not prepared to let election time pass without voting for some party.

This was the body of responsible, but disenchanted, voters that the Third Party was aiming for. Its policies were striking right to the hearts of many middle and working class voters, with revolutionary ideas about reducing tax burdens and radical plans to help the poor and infirm with crippling medical bills.

The country was Nathan's oyster, or so it seemed as that summer turned to fall. There were just three months left for electioneering. Three short months in which to pull it off. The pressure was on.

Nathan's team, headed by the dour, unflappable Newt Ludlow, burnt the midnight oil, discussing tactics, resources and public relations, to the point of exhaustion. Despite the fact that he'd got an injection of capital through selling his law practice partnership, Nathan was still financially much worse off than either of the other candidates, the millionaires Carter and Reagan. In consequence he knew that every dollar in his campaign budget must be made to count.

The team mapped out what they considered to be a reasonable achievable itinerary within the available timescale. They were unanimous in considering it vital to gain votes in the South. Yet

The Chameleon Candidate

they knew they had neither the time nor the resources to cover all the Southern States.

A compromise was reached. They would concentrate on Mississippi, Nathan's home State. He should have a head start there and a potential power base. With many of his policies geared to the economy of that area, together with his well-publicized record on Northern Civil Rights, the team gambled on the chance that once campaigning began in earnest, the good news should filter through to the other Southern States.

Days on end were spent in working on vital public relations, drafting and re-drafting press releases and flyers, to highlight Nathan's new 'Mississippi Boy Makes Good' image.

Chapter Sixteen

Concentrating on going to Mississippi bored into Nathan's brain, dripping away like acid. He had become convinced it was crucial to the success of his campaign to get there before it was too late, to establish a power base.

It was all becoming highly significant, and he couldn't resist a surge of pride. After all he had been, not so many years ago, part of a poor white trash family, existing like tens of thousands of others, in a tarpaper shack on the banks of the Mississippi. Soon he was to be campaigning among his own kind as a presidential candidate, and in doing this, he would be mixing with the most influential in the land. By anyone's standards, that was a rags to riches story, he thought.

But once this short-lived euphoria had settled down inside him, he began to reason that American history was already peppered with similar success stories. In any case, he was still guilt-ridden and saddened. He was burdened with a sadness that would never go away, and which would inevitably erode the gilt from any gingerbread that might be on offer.

After the euphoria came the doubts. He began to wonder: did the folk of Idle Winds know about the fate of his family? If they did, would they blame him for not being there, the same way that Julius had blamed him? There would still be people about, folk who knew his background, who would put two and two together. Perhaps they too would accuse him of seeing to himself at the expense of everyone else? He knew it was not true. Quite the reverse, but he couldn't expect folk to know about the impossible circumstances in which his family found itself, or that he as a small boy had neither choice nor control about being packed off to New York.

Perhaps he should have tried harder to contact his family during those formative years spent up north. Just because they hadn't made it easy for him, was no excuse. He was the educated one. He was the one with a modern communication system at his fingertips.

Well it was all far too late now. He was not usually one for indulging in post mortems, considering them to be depressing, time wasting exercises. Yet here he was right in the middle of a significant one. He must shake off these negative thoughts. All he knew was his mind was set on going to Mississippi. When he got there he would have to take the consequences, good or bad.

Now was the time to give the Presidency his best shot and leave it at that. He would use all his considerable powers of oratory, coupled with all the concentration his incisive legal mind was capable of, in his attempts to make his dream come true.

But despite himself his self-analysis rumbled on. He would have to try to be fair to himself, otherwise he was in danger of sinking again under a lack of confidence. That would be fatal.

The bottom line had to be acknowledged. He had achieved a great deal. Apart from Aunt Nessie, who'd been both mother and guardian to him, and Mayo Cleveland, his mentor, he'd gotten to his present position virtually unaided.

He was aware that many of his peers from high school and university had by now reaped the benefits accruing from normal family structures, no matter how rough or basic these might have been. Such strengths and stabilities were denied him. Consequently, he had to forge his own. He'd had to develop his own values and understanding of human nature as he went along.

He was not an all-rounder, he knew that well enough. Folk would say, if they knew, that he had let his family down. Not the other way around, as he had been so tempted to think until he had embarked on his recent round of soul searching. At least now he was mature enough to face down the ghosts of the past, and to begin to admit that he could, indeed should, have done more for his family. The pigeons had come home to roost. His unusual upbringing had

Sixteen

undoubtedly taken its toll!

All that long summer of 1980, Newt Ludlow, Margaret Merrylee (his deputy) and the others in Nathan's dedicated campaign team, worked ruthlessly behind the scenes. Their mission was to put in place a machine so smooth, so efficient, that once their boss was in the rumble seat, he could sit back and be driven on to victory. Ludlow had succeeded already in setting up a small campaign team based in Natchez. This would act as their operational headquarters to reach into other Southern States.

A good deal of toe dipping in the Mississippi waters had elicited positive feedback for support for the Third Party. Natchez, chosen purposely for its geographical position, was sufficiently far south to allow the team to tap into Louisiana and Arkansas. The hope was that enthusiasm for Nathan, already bubbling up in Mississippi, would almost certainly overflow into adjoining States.

The end of August and barely two clear months left until the November elections. Carter, the most conservative President since Grover Cleveland, a hundred years before, was hanging in by the skin of his teeth. In the Republican camp, Reagan, with money to burn on his campaign, was already flexing his muscles in anticipation of a decisive victory. But Beauregarde, or 'The Mugwump', as he was beginning to be called by the media, felt more and more that there were sufficient middle ground voters to be scooped up by his party, allowing him a real chance at victory.

On Ludlow's advice, Nathan agreed to set up his Third Party Convention in Natchez during a weekend in mid-September. This convention was of vital importance to test the credibility of their campaign. In Ludlow's eyes it would be very much a make-or-break weekend, to ensure that all systems were in working order. And, now that their election train had well and truly left the station, to convince voters it meant serious business, and should be listened to.

Since April, after an authoritative article appeared in the New York Times, written by veteran political correspondent Faz Baylin, the media had swung its sights around to zone in on the up and coming Third Party. Consequently, Ludlow knew the eyes and ears of the world would be on this convention. In particular, all eyes would be on the new Senator, a man who fancied his chances against Carter and Reagan.

For months, media hype had indicated that perhaps the time was ripe to fill the vacuum with such a 'David' who might just be able to slip between the two established, but tarnished, 'Goliaths'.

One evening in early September, Nathan, Hebe Blantyre (his driver) and Harper Turnbull, the FBI bodyguard assigned to him, set off from New York in Nathan's large black Chevrolet. They were headed for campaign headquarters in Natchez. Doug Madison, the agent appointed by Ludlow to look after the affairs of the Third Party in the South, had managed to acquire office accommodation in the center of Natchez for the duration of the campaign. As time was becoming important, Nathan decided to drive to Mississippi as quickly as possible, with the minimum of stops.

In the early hours of the morning of the second of September, some fifty kilometers north of Jackson, the vehicle was involved in a horrific accident.

...The sleek, black Chevrolet must have been busting a gut. Patrolman Toni Rossi, of the Mississippi State Police, came upon it suddenly as he rounded a bend on his motorcycle. The vehicle had ploughed into the parapet of a bridge. It now lay, at a crazy, drunken angle, protruding onto the highway. The high-pitched hiss of steam still gushing from the fractured radiator indicated the accident was recent.

Zebra stripes of light were already lazering the sky from the east as Rossi glanced at his watch; it said 05:00 hours. The highway illumination reflected thick black tire marks where the driver had braked in a final desperate attempt at control.

Rossi cursed silently as he brought his machine to a juddering halt. He propped it on its stand on the hard shoulder. This was his last half hour of duty. He could have done without this. Accidents always spell work, and by

Sixteen

the look of this one it was truly 'molto sfavorevole'.
    He approached the car with a sinking feeling, observing the New York license plate. There were bound to be casualties, almost certainly fatalities. The force of the crash had concertinaed the vehicle, ripping open the hood, so now it yawned wide like the jaws of some giant doomed crocodile.
    The driver's door had been flung across to the other side of the highway, thus allowing a view of the carnage within. The sight that presented itself made even the battle-hardened cop catch his breath. The driver was dead. One glance was sufficient; his jugular vein had been severed by a chunk of windshield. Now his glazed eyes stared unseeingly at the sunroof.
    Likewise, the man in the passenger seat was lifeless. The angle of his head indicated a broken neck. A further glance told Rossi he was an FBI agent. He could smell them a mile off. The man's badge inside his coat confirmed it.
    But it was the passenger in the rear who really focused Rossi's attention. His tall bulk was sprawled across the seat. Immediately his dress set him apart as someone of consequence: silk tie, white silk shirt, Italian gray suit. Rossi could always spot the Italian cut.
    Carefully he raised the head for a better look. The face had been badly cut by windshield glass and pieces of dashboard that had disintegrated. Despite the blood, something about the face jarred a memory cell within the cop. He felt for a pulse, eventually locating a tiny flutter.
    Instinct told Rossi he was onto something big. This was no ordinary accident. An unusual feeling of inadequacy engulfed him as he withdrew from the vehicle and hurried back to his machine to radio for help…

Nathan was rushed by ambulance to hospital in Jackson. Once there he went straight into intensive care.

When Nathan hadn't arrived at the Grand Hotel, Natchez that morning, Ludlow became alarmed. By midday, when he still hadn't put in an appearance, he telephoned the police. They gave him details of the accident.

Dreadfully shaken, Ludlow gathered together his team and broke the news. For what seemed like a lifetime they sat huddled around the table, saying little, attempting to take in the implications of this tragedy.

The police told Ludlow what the hospital had told them. Nathan was in a deep coma. His life was hanging by a thread. There was no guarantee that he would emerge from the coma and, if he did, there was a strong possibility that he could be brain damaged.

Fighting back feelings of panic, Ludlow struggled for a semblance of control. He gave the team fifteen minutes to compose themselves, to prepare for a brain bashing session. One thing they were all agreed on, secrecy about the crash must be maintained at all costs.

Ludlow made some urgent telephone calls. He discovered that Ray Jordan, the chief of police in Jackson, was a strong advocate of the party. He told Ludlow that in his opinion Nathan Beauregarde appeared to be just what was needed as President. He agreed to hush up Nathan's involvement in the accident for as long as possible, '...in the interests of good political sense...' he said. Toni Rossi, the cop at the scene of the accident, was already on their side, although they had no way of knowing that.

Then, surprisingly, and much to Ludlow's relief, the FBI agreed to co-operate in the cover up. Their agent Turnbull, a New Yorker, was buried with the minimum of fuss. With the respective agencies adopting, quite unexpectedly, such a positive and helpful attitude, Ludlow felt that he could put pressure on the hospital administration in Jackson to follow suit. But the main problem, that of Nathan's absence during such a vital period, still had to be addressed

It was at this point, when he began to think about his leader's absence, that Ludlow had to use all his inner resources not to succumb to the hopelessness he felt welling up inside him. The party they had created and loved, the party they had worked so hard for, and had such high hopes for, could be on the verge of extinction before it even had a chance to run. So near, yet so far. With the main actor off stage, what use was the production? They wouldn't even make it through the first night!

Sixteen

As he sat gazing at the faces around the table, all relying on him to wave a magic wand to make everything all right, a tiny germ of a crazy idea began to work its way into Ludlow's brain. He recalled one day earlier that summer, when Nathan, in an unusually expansive mood, had confided in him that he had an identical twin brother. A great disappointment to him, he was doing time in prison in Alabama. It was the word 'identical' that now lingered in Ludlow's mind.

He began to write on a piece of paper – the fors' and againsts', something he always did when he was trying to come to an important decision. As he developed his plan, he was greatly heartened in his resolve by the fact that the authorities appeared to be on his side in the cover-up.

He took a deep breath, looked hard at each face in turn, trying to predict their reactions to his rescue plan. In defense of what he was about to suggest, he knew as sure as there was breath in his body, that all of them had committed themselves fully to the success of the party. A cruel and unexpected blow now threatened to blow their good ship hopeful out of the water. This must not be allowed to happen. Religious man that he was, he said a silent prayer, then blurted out his plan.

Chapter Seventeen

Ludlow had made one more telephone call before he aired what must have been the craziest rescue plan of all time. He telephoned the Alabama State Prison to ascertain if Julius Beauregarde was still an inmate. To his great relief, he was informed that Beauregarde had been out on parole for the past month. This now left the way clear for Ludlow to tell his team what was on his mind. Clutching at straws, as they were, they bought it.

Ludlow would proceed to Alabama. There he would outline his plan to Julius. The deal was that he stood in for his brother during the vital convention weekend and, if necessary, right up to election time, and beyond. They would expect Julius to do as he was told, to make real and strenuous efforts to act the part of his brother, in all respects.

In return the party was offering him a one-off payment of fifty thousand dollars. No questions asked. Once the need for his presence had ceased, he would be expected to disappear and get on with his life.

The main aim of this plan was to buy valuable time to allow for Nathan's recovery. In the event he didn't recover, and either died, or did not emerge from the coma, it would still buy time at the primaries. It would allow for meaningful exposure of the new Third Party to the electorate, to let them see what it could do for them. Without Nathan's presence, they were all agreed that the party would wither and die on the vine.

It was the only plan Ludlow could think of. No one else could produce any ideas. So, illegal and riddled with risk as it was, it appeared to be their only chance of success.

Leaving campaign affairs in the hands of his deputy, Margaret

Seventeen

Merrylee, Ludlow flew to Montgomery. Once there, he would beard the lion in his den, put the proposition to Julius, and see what the response was. But he must resolve it within the next twenty-four hours.

On the plane, during the short journey, doubts began to assail him. He had taken an awful lot on face value, on Nathan's few words about the existence of a twin. Were they really identical? Would Julius be interested in the crazy proposition? If so, could he be coached adequately in the role during the short time left? Most of all, would he be capable of carrying the whole thing off? There would be no time to put another plan into operation, assuming that he could even think of one!

At Montgomery Airport, Ludlow took a taxi to the address given to him by the prison authorities. It turned out to be a seedy boarding house, one from a list used by the parole board. A middle aged, unkempt woman opened the door.

Yes, Beauregarde was in. 'Who wants him?'

'A friend of the family.'

The woman led the way down a tatty corridor, stopping at the end. She knocked on a door, and moved off.

The door was opened by a mirror image of Nathan, with the exception of his hair, which was longer and black. Julius was also wearing a villainous looking moustache, resembling dead man's fingers on a crab.

Ludlow introduced himself.

Julius gazed at him blankly, and without enthusiasm.

'May I?' Ludlow waved towards the solitary chair.

Julius nodded. By now he was sitting on the bed.

Ludlow sat down. Already he was beginning to feel unnerved. Julius hadn't spoken, and he was finding it more difficult to start the dialogue than he thought.

Finally he spoke. 'I have what I'm sure you'll consider to be a most unusual proposition to put to you. I do hope you'll hear me out?'

The Chameleon Candidate

There was no reaction from the bed.

Speaking slowly, Ludlow outlined the plan in as much detail as he considered fit. There was still no reaction, even when he explained that he was doing this because Nathan, his twin brother, was at that moment critically ill in hospital. It was only when money was mentioned that the man on the bed looked up.

'How much?'

'Fifty thousand dollars.'

Only then did Julius begin to speak, in a voice in pitch and timbre that was uncannily like his brother's. Understandably, it contained drawled southern pronunciation, whereas Nathan had acquired the more incisive tone of the native New Yorker.

As Julius finally entered into dialogue, Ludlow wasted no time in getting a line on him. He knew a person can't really be assessed until they speak. But there was something Ludlow had not been prepared for; Julius's reaction to his brother. There was a deep, undisguised resentment, quite disturbing in its intensity. He knew then there was no question that Julius Beauregarde would accept the deal for any other motive than money. Loyalty to his brother just didn't enter into it.

This didn't worry Ludlow unduly. In fact, he understood. Probably he would have done the same thing in his place. The cash was very tempting for any jailbird. It was a once in a lifetime opportunity to acquire that sort of amount legitimately.

Warming to his theme, and in anticipation of Julius's acceptance, Ludlow introduced his list of demands. They were all part of the deal, to which Julius would be expected to adhere. Firstly his presence was required at the forthcoming convention. Ludlow and the others in the team would do their best to keep face-to-face contact, with either the media or potential voters, to a minimum. They would shield him as much as they could. A time limit could not be put on their agreement. It would end when, in Ludlow's opinion, the job was done. Then the money would be paid and Julius would disappear.

Seventeen

Ludlow had brought a recording of Nathan's voice while making a speech. He played this to Julius, asking him to imitate his northern tones. Julius, his interest captured now, gave a very fair imitation.

Ludlow was beginning to relax. He was feeling pleased with the way the interview had gone. He was delighted with the similarity of the brothers. Most of all, he was convinced Julius did have the necessary intelligence to carry the mission through.

'Well, what do you think?' he said.

Julius stared at the ceiling for a while, drawing deeply on a cigarette. Finally he looked at Ludlow. 'Yeah. OK.'

The relief on Ludlow's face was stark.

'There's just one thing though,' said Julius.

'Yes?'

'The money. Half now, the rest when the job's done.'

That had not been Ludlow's intention. He was caught unawares. If he agreed to this he'd be taking a risk that Julius would disappear with the money, leaving them all high and dry. But he was desperate. He had come too far to be defeated now. In any case, he was already taking the risk of a lifetime.

'All right, a quarter now. But you'll have to wait till we get to Natchez.'

'OK. What the hell!' Julius agreed.

'There's just one more thing,' Ludlow said, pointing to Julius's cigarette.

'What?'

'None of those. Not in public anyway. Your brother doesn't smoke.'

Julius stared at him.

There was one more matter to be attended to before they flew back to Natchez. The prison authorities had to be satisfied that Julius could be safely released into Ludlow's care. Under the terms of his parole, Julius was not allowed to be more than ten miles from Montgomery at any given time, let alone in another state. This had to be organized without revealing the real reason Julius was needed. The fewer folk who knew about the plans for the impersonation, the better, as far as Ludlow was concerned. Persuasive when he needed to be, Ludlow got them to agree, provided Julius telephoned his parole officer each day.

Later that evening Julius was installed in the penthouse suite in the Grand Hotel, Natchez, booked in under his brother's name. The big deception had begun.

It wasn't too long before Julius found himself enjoying every minute of his new role. The transformation from jailbird to Presidential candidate had been as swift as it was unbelievable – and, so far, painless. He loved the luxury of the suite, particularly the bathroom, where he spent hours each day preening himself.

The moustache went. A gray rinse was put in his hair, to make it more like Nathan's. Ludlow was delighted to find, apart from some work on his voice, and practice in cultivating gestures Nathan had made his own in public, that was pretty much it. To all intents and purposes, Julius Beauregarde was his brother.

Quickly Julius found himself developing a newfound confidence, cockiness even. More so, perhaps, than Ludlow was comfortable with. Within days he had read himself into the role. In his own eyes, Julius was the real man. He knew his brother had always been a wimp. He certainly was when they were youngsters, and from what he could gather, he was still the one with no bone in his cock. As he drifted around the palatial suite in his new designer crimson smoking jacket, fondling the beautiful furniture, pausing frequently to admire his reflection in the mirrors, he knew he would find this life hard to give up.

Already his mind had performed the necessary adjustment. He had convinced himself that he, not his brother, was the one who'd been born for all this. He reveled in the respect the hotel staff gave him. He found little difficulty in persuading himself that his whole life had been nothing less than a preparation for this moment, and what was to come.

In his present euphoric state of mind, Julius ignored his almost

Seventeen

complete lack of formal education, his total lack of political knowledge, or even basic grasp of current affairs. He was still the man for the job! It was meant to be that Nathan had put himself out of the picture, Julius hoped for good!

True to his word, Ludlow paid over the quarter fee to Julius. Distrusting banks, never having occasion to use them in the past, Julius kept his money in the security safe in his suite, taking fistfuls of notes out from time to time when he needed them.

This arrangement suited Ludlow admirably. He had no desire for Julius, with his track record, to open a bank account, which would inevitably attract all kinds of questions. Within a day, Julius had spent five thousand dollars, most of it on clothes and jewelry. This included a Cartier wristwatch.

'After all, ah has ta look the part!' he told Ludlow.

Bobby Blackstock plumped up the pillows, kissed his wife tenderly goodbye and set off for his work as a bell hop in the Grand Hotel.

It had been a grueling two years. Kara, his beloved wife, had cancer of the ovaries. It was an aggressive disease, and it was terminal. Already she had begun her long slow walk to a painful death. Bobby couldn't bear it. The long months spent in hospital having treatment that hadn't worked had brought him to the brink of bankruptcy and close to a nervous breakdown.

But he had to be strong for her. He had to remain cheerful. He couldn't let her see how dreadfully worried he was. Now, in the final months of her life, Blackstock had begged the hospital to be allowed to look after her at home. Ultimately they agreed. So all the dreadful wires and tubes her poor wasted body had been set about with were dismantled, and he accompanied her home in an ambulance.

Now all he had to do was administer her relentless daily intake of pills. Brown pills, yellow pills, white pills, black pills, square pills, round pills, even orange pills. All in the same shaped bottles, only the instructions on the labels were different. Several times during the last month alone, when the pain had become unbearable, she begged him to give her an overdose, to end her suffering. But he couldn't – he just couldn't. His strict Baptist upbringing wouldn't allow it.

All of a sudden, for Newt Ludlow, things somehow seemed to be fitting into a kind of manageable, if crazy, jigsaw puzzle. When he'd first conceived his plan, he had hesitated to think too deeply about the consequences if it was rumbled. Yet, despite everything, so far as he could see, things were working out pretty smoothly. So smoothly, in fact, that he began to wonder whether there was some dimension he had not thought about, some dark, gaping fissure just around the corner, waiting to swallow them up.

That first day, Ludlow had introduced Julius to his little campaign team: Margaret Merrylee, his deputy, a chunky determined blonde from Wichita, Dermod Mahoney, an Irish American of Ludlow's own vintage, an experienced veteran of the campaign trail and Virgil Clarke, a young New York law graduate and protégé of Nathan. Understandably, they were anxious to test out their new acquisition. They wanted to assess his voice, his looks, his attitude, his fortitude, and, most of all, his commitment. They too had nailed their colors to the mast. The point of no return had been reached. There would be no turning back for any of them.

Warming to his theme in front of the ready made audience, and warming to a job he hoped would become permanent; Julius gave a very fair rendering of his hated brother. In this scenario he played down the hatred that had been so obvious to Ludlow in the prison. He was convincing. He was playing the game. He was anxious to impress his new employers. For their part, they were more relieved than they could say. They were happier in their minds about the gigantic bluff than they had thought possible. With only forty-eight hours left until the convention, however, a frightening amount still remained to be done.

Chapter Eighteen

Only forty-eight hours to the convention. Every time he thought about it, a shudder worked its way up Ludlow's spine. There was so much at stake. The future was based on the craziest of plans.

If the impersonation was discovered, many people would be in serious trouble. He could barely believe they had got as far as they had with the plot. The fact that so many people in high places were prepared to look the other way to help in the cover up, gave Ludlow a feeling of pride. It meant they were sticking their necks out for Nathan and the Third Party.

Never before in the history of America, so far as Ludlow was aware, and he knew his political history, had a Presidential Candidate ever been impersonated in this manner. If they got away with it, it would truly be a miracle.

The convention alone would be make or break, never mind the elections. Would their train still be on the rails by November? All the whole crazy house of cards needed was one investigative journalist to delve and poke, then spill the beans. They would be finished.

During his agonizing before he decided to involve Julius, Ludlow had considered running ahead without Nathan. But, as the founder, he was such an integral part of the organization that he quickly discarded the idea. A brand new Third Party, on her maiden voyage without her captain – forget it!

Julius didn't like dull days, not if he could possibly help it. God alone knew he had endured enough of them in prison, or after recovering from being drugged out of his mind in Berkeley or San Francisco. After all, he'd reasoned, that was why he took drugs in the first place – to cut out the drabness and dullness of ordinary life. Looking back, his whole life seemed to have been beset with dull days, from his poverty stricken childhood in Mississippi, where there never was money for anything, right up to his lonely teenage days on the ranch in Montgomery, where nobody wanted to know him. He had never felt part of anything. Was it any wonder he went off the rails?

Now, for the first time in his life, he felt in control of his destiny, in control of the dullness, or otherwise, in his life. One of the many reasons why he was desperate to hang on to this opportunity to enrich his life, an opportunity ironically presented to him by his hated brother, was to ensure that he didn't have any more dull days. He was convinced dull days were for no account folk who were incapable of making their days on earth anything else. He resolved never again to be a no account person. He smiled at the thought that Ludlow would discover soon enough that his temporary employee had become permanent. Now that he was a long way from the twilight world of drug addiction, he had no intention of returning there. Julius Beauregarde was out to secure his own golden dream.

Despite Julius's excellent start, Ludlow and his team had their work cut out in the few hours left before the convention to polish and hone his performance. One of the disadvantages of television in this particular case was that Nathan had already enjoyed considerable TV coverage during the summer. As a result, his image had been seen already on screen in the majority of American homes.

Ludlow prepared an aide-memoir for Julius to keep with him at all times. He kept it as simple as possible. It consisted of a series of headings, written in large letters, so that Julius could read them. It listed the kind of questions and answers he expected Julius would have to deal with. He also put together a brief history of the party, its aims and mission statement, focusing on Nathan's excellent

Eighteen

track record on Civil Rights.

Now it was all down to Julius. Ludlow was relieved to find that, far from his initial enthusiasm wearing thin, it had become reinforced. Confidence was just oozing out of him.

There was no doubt, once money was mentioned, Julius had entered into the spirit of the conspiracy from the outset with determination, energy and even humor. If he had been a mind reader, Ludlow would have seen the dangerous road this enthusiasm was taking. But, as things were, he was simply content to note that all appeared to be panning out well.

The next morning Bobby Blackstock, smart in his gold braided blue uniform and pillbox hat, lingered at the reception desk in the Grand Hotel. He always did this first thing to find out what jobs needed to be done, or which guests needed attention. Eliza Power, the colored receptionist, beckoned to him. He was to go up to the penthouse suite, taking a bottle of champagne in an ice bucket, and the morning papers.

The guest's name was Nathan Beauregarde, the politician. Minutes later Blackstock was at the door of the suite. He had to knock several times before it was opened. Finally, Julius stood there, fresh from the shower, hair wet, a modest towel wrapped around his waist.

'Mr Beauregarde?'

'Uh huh.'

'You rang, sir?'

'Oh yeah, set them down on the table.'

Julius stepped aside to let the colored man into the room. As he walked past him, something clicked in Blackstock's brain. The name, Beauregarde, was familiar. Of course, the Beauregarde twins! He had more reason to remember them than most! So this was Nathan, the nice guy. The gentle little boy had grown into a man. Now that he thought about it, he had heard he was a Senator and running for President. But no one had taken the trouble to tell him he was a guest in the hotel. Still, there was something gnawing in the back of Blackstock's mind. He couldn't put a finger on it.

He took his time about setting down the champagne and arranging the papers on the table. His memory was working overtime, away back to childhood to his experience of the identical twins, as different in character as chalk from cheese. One had been kind and thoughtful, the other nasty and vicious.

Bobby Blackstock had a good memory. He'd always prided himself on it. He never had to take notes of messages or jobs to be done about the hotel, he always remembered. So this was Nathan standing in front of him. He looked into his face as he turned away from the table. There was a harshness of expression that didn't seem quite right in the face that he remembered.

Julius was staring at him. He turned away. He'd been there long enough. Already he was imagining too much. After all, it was over thirty years ago. A great deal of water had flowed under the bridge since they were boys. Perhaps life had not been good for Nathan? Perhaps it was executive stress, he'd read about how it affected folk in high places. Yes, that must be it. A man such as he must be under an awful lot of stress all the time.

He backed towards the door and was about to close it behind him when he saw it. There was a small purple scar pushing its way above the skimpy towel. Beauregarde must have reached for a hand towel by mistake in his hurry to open the door, it was not big enough to conceal the scar.

My God, the scar! His scar! The very scar he'd made on Julius all those years ago, done in retaliation after Julius and Levi Hazzard held him down and circumcised him on the banks of the Mississippi. It must be that scar. It was in the right place. It was too much of a coincidence for it not to be! A paralyzing fear engulfed Bobby as he stepped backwards into the corridor. What in the name of the Almighty was going on?

So the Beauregarde in that room was an imposter! Blackstock knew beyond a shadow of a doubt the guest was Julius, not

Eighteen

Nathan. Furthermore, and this was truly frightening, he was the only person in the world who could know it. As he traveled to the ground floor in the elevator, his mind was in fearful turmoil. He had to think, to work all this out. Why was Julius impersonating his brother? If it was a plot, then others must be in on it. But who, and how many?

The one good thing that appeared to be in his favor was that he was fairly sure Beauregarde had not recognized him. That put him in a stronger position; he had the element of surprise on his side. But what to do about it? After what seemed like a lifetime, lunch break time came.

In recent weeks, because he had been so worried about Kara – there was no one else to look after her – Blackstock had taken to going back to the apartment during his short break, to check on her.

He let himself in, walked quietly to her bedroom and gazed down at her poor worn face, a face once so pretty, so vibrant, before the ravages of the dreadfully cruel disease had taken their toll.

He got her a cool drink, gave her the pills and changed the television channel to her favorite lunchtime soap. The big television was her only comfort now that her eyes were so bad. She was unable to read for any length of time. He bathed her forehead, held her hand and gently chatted about this and that.

As he talked his eyes took in the tiny bare room. He knew he had done well enough in life, working his way up from message boy to senior bellhop in the prestigious Grand Hotel. For a while, when they were first married and Kara was working, they enjoyed a good lifestyle. But all that was gone. All his savings and resources were long since spent on doctor's bills. These days he could barely muster the rent. There was so much she needed. So much he reckoned he could do to make her last few months on this earth more comfortable, if only he had the money.

Money! Suddenly he had an idea. He would blackmail Julius

The Chameleon Candidate

Beauregarde! He was in a unique position to do so. Never before in his God-fearing life would he have contemplated such a thing. Even now, he wouldn't be doing it for himself. But he was quite desperate for money, and besides, Julius owed him. By God, yes he owed him! He spent a sleepless night pondering on how best to set about his plan.

By the time the first streaks of light made their presence felt in the dawn sky, he had made up his mind. Now that he knew Beauregarde was in politics, he had spent some time reading the papers. He read about the convention due shortly. He put two and two together and worked out that it must be very important for this new party to have Nathan at the helm, otherwise they wouldn't have ventured on anything so risky as an impersonation. Something must have happened to Nathan.

Bobby would demand a one-off payment of fifty thousand dollars. He would do this by the simple process of pushing a note under Julius's door. A note which would contain sufficient information to alert him as to whom he was dealing with, and threatening that, if it was not complied with, the whistle would be blown. The cash was to be left at reception in clean one hundred dollar bills in a plain envelope with his name on it. In that way Bobby Blackstock could distance himself from Julius. He knew what a violent and vicious little boy he had been. That aspect of his character could hardly have changed!

He thought carefully about the wording of the note, experimenting with several before he got it right. Then he slipped it under Julius's door.

Blackstock was correct in his assumption that Julius had no idea as to his identity. Consequently the demand note came as a bolt from the sky. His first reaction was to dismiss it as the work of a crank. But the more he thought about it, the more he realized that he couldn't afford to write it off. The information contained in it could only have come from one source. No one else could possibly have

Eighteen

written that note.

He was trapped, and he knew it. What desperate fucking luck, and when things were going so well! He couldn't confide in anyone. Ludlow, the fixer, couldn't fix this.

It all began to flood back. His childhood in Idle Winds and the mild mannered little coon whom he hated with intensity just because he was there and he was black. Perhaps he had been unkind to him. But he wasn't the only poor white trash kid who'd indulged in nigger baiting, no siree, not by a long shot.

Momentarily he thought about Levi and all the other kids he'd been brought up with. What had happened to them all? Now, all these years later, the little bastard Blackstock was obviously hell bent on revenge. But hadn't he done that already? Julius fingered his scar and cursed the hand towel that had not covered it. But it was all too late now. Something would have to be done, and soon.

For a time he paced the room like a caged lion, with every step cursing his bad luck. Ludlow was due inside the hour for a final briefing before the convention. He needed to have a plan in place to deal with Blackstock before that, if only for his own peace of mind.

There was a knock at the door, his breakfast on a tray. His mind churned all the while he was eating. No inspiration came.

The maid returned to take the tray away. After she'd gone he stretched out in a chair. He reached for the notes Ludlow had given him. He must steady himself. He must concentrate.

After half an hour of this, he needed air. He opened the sliding door leading to the balcony and stepped out. Some good, fresh Natchez air should do the trick.

For a while he gazed over the rooftops of the city to the river in the far distance. That great gray ribbon of the Father of Waters, the great granddaddy of all North American rivers, measuring over two thousand miles from its headwaters in Minnesota to its outflow into the Louisiana deltas. He was standing there for two purposes, to clear his head and to seek inspiration as to how to get out of his new problem.

The Chameleon Candidate

The problem was to be resolved sooner than he thought. He heard a noise below him. He looked down onto the top of Bobby Blackstock's head! He couldn't believe it. His prayers had been answered. Blackstock was on the balcony of the room immediately below him and, like him, was taking some air.

What a bellhop was doing there, Julius had no idea, the room must be vacant, or the occupants away for the day. But none of that mattered. In that split second he knew what he must do...

Thinking little about the consequences, Julius propelled himself out of his room. He checked that the coast was clear and raced down the stairs. This was quicker than using the elevator and involved less chance of being seen. Stealthily he moved up to the door of the room.

It was partly open. It was now or never.

Silently, Julius moved across the thick pile carpet and through the open sliding door to the balcony. Blackstock had not moved. At the last moment he turned.

Too late.

Julius lunged forward. Always physically strong, he quickly overpowered the unsuspecting man. With one heave he lifted Bobby off his feet and pushed him over the balcony rail. With a terrified scream, Bobby Blackstock began his last journey from seven floors up to the ground below. He landed on the roof of a car with a sickening thud. A thud Julius heard quite clearly. Now was the time to get out. Still his luck held.

Upstairs again, breathing heavily, he closed the door of the suite behind him. All this had taken less than five minutes. He hadn't seen a soul.

He resisted the temptation to pour himself a large bourbon. Even by his standards, it was a trifle early, and there was work to be done. Grabbing his papers, he moved out onto his balcony. Already composed after the murder, he leaned casually on the rail watching the commotion below. Two minutes later Ludlow knocked and entered.

Eighteen

Shortly after nine o'clock Eliza Power had called Bobby Blackstock's name over the hotel intercom. He was needed right away. The occupants of a room on the seventh floor were complaining about the plumbing. On their way out for the day, they had left their key at reception, expecting the matter to be cleared up on their return. There was no sign of Hank Busby, the hotel's maintenance engineer. Could Bobby investigate and report back?

Ten minutes later Bobby Blackstock's broken body was found spread-eagled over the top of a resident's car in the hotel car park. Ludlow joined Julius on the balcony. Together they stared down at the fuss below.

'What a terrible thing. Must be either accident, or perhaps suicide?' Ludlow said.

'Suppose,' was all the response Julius made.

Then they heard the sirens. Ambulance and police were converging on the spot almost together. Even from his vantage point eight floors above, Julius could see that Bobby was dead. That was all that mattered. The threat was lifted. The incident closed. No one would ever know.

That afternoon was a success. Sunny and bright, the walkabout in Natchez went off better than Ludlow had dared to hope. Julius was truly in his element. He either answered questions directly, or fielded others that came his way skillfully, like the professional he was fast becoming.

It was Saturday, the 20th of September, almost three weeks since Nathan's near fatal accident, and one day before the all-important convention. Inside that time Julius's whole life had changed.

The convention went well, smoothly and professionally, with no hitches. Ludlow need not have worried, the re-born Julius rose magnificently to the occasion. The faithful came to hear him in droves. It achieved what Ludlow had hoped and prayed for. That weekend the Third Party's credibility rose by leaps and bounds. Julius had the bit firmly between his teeth. There would be no

The Chameleon Candidate

stopping him now.

There was just one clear month before elections in November. A vast amount of canvassing still had to be done outside Mississippi. The feedback was good, it was positive. Word was spreading through the Gulf States about the sense in voting for Beauregarde. Ludlow and his team were working an eighteen-hour day.

September turned to October. The Third Party was on a roll, gaining momentum all the time. Each day brought fresh interest in the party, all at the expense of the main parties.

Each morning Julius awoke, his adrenalin flowing at the thought of what victories that day would bring. Nothing must be allowed to de-rail his train now. He had never been so happy, so secure, so involved in meaningful business than he was during those heady days of that fall.

Never had he dreamt it possible that he could be the recipient of such devotion and interest from an expectant public.

Before this, he'd had to resort to notoriety in order to bring him the attention his nature craved. Now here it was, handed to him on a plate, everywhere, inside the hotel, outside in cities and towns, in the countryside, even networking its way into other states.

He had erased successfully from his mind everything that he didn't wish to think about. This included matters such as the Bobby Blackstock murder, and the fact that he was still only a caretaker candidate. There was only one Beauregarde – and he was it.

Chapter Nineteen

On the seventeenth of October, forty-four days after the horrendous accident that had been within a whisker of ending his life, Nathan Beauregarde awoke. Without any warning, he came out of the coma that doctors had thought, privately, was irreversible. From that point, he slowly fought his way back to life.

It was two days before he could talk, and a further two before he was strong enough to sit up in bed. A miracle indeed.

On the fifth day he sought details of the accident, and was told both his companions had died. He asked for a telephone. He put through a call to his campaign manager in Natchez. Ludlow was in the hotel at the time the call came through. Seven days previously he had contacted the hospital to inquire about Nathan's progress. At that time there was no change. He was still in a deep coma. Now this call. Another bolt from the blue and, if he was truthful, the last thing on earth he needed.

Nathan's voice was weak, but unmistakable. He inquired how things had been going along without him. There was a long silence, the longest in Ludlow's life.

Finally he spoke, telling his boss in measured tones what had happened and what action he had been forced to take.

After the initial shock of hearing Nathan's voice had subsided, the irony of the situation began to penetrate Ludlow's mind. A few, unbelievably short weeks ago, he was literally desperate without Nathan's presence. Now that very presence threatened to wreck all his carefully laid plans. He had embarked on a hair-brained and totally illegal mission to replace Nathan with his brother, a man he'd never met, never really believing it could possibly work. At best he'd viewed it as a breathing space for his hard-pressed team and, if indeed the brothers were identical, to keep the prying eyes of the media at a distance.

Now the irony lay in the fact that his plan had been so very successful. The price for that success would soon be revealed to him.

Over the past weeks it had become obvious that Julius possessed the spark, the style of humor and delivery and the panache, that his quieter brother just did not have. Quite simply it boiled down to the fact that Julius was a natural. The public loved him, and he reached out to them. Nathan, on the other hand, despite his brains and qualifications, tended to wait till folk came to him.

The telephone conversation now reached the point that Ludlow was dreading. Nathan wanted back in the action.

Ludlow could feel his heart pounding as he tried to prepare his answers for what he knew was coming.

'Surely the party must be losing out badly without my presence Newt. I don't know how you've managed at all!' Nathan was saying.

He went on to congratulate Ludlow on having the initiative to use his brother in a temporary capacity. It had obviously bought some valuable time. He just hoped Julius had not let the side down.

'Yeah, he probably would be OK for a very short time,' continued Nathan, referring to his brother. 'He certainly has the cheek. But that's all over now. Pay him off Newt, whatever you agreed, that's OK by me. But get him off the scene. I'll be back within three days to take over the reins again.'

Ludlow's heart sank. He knew it wouldn't be as simple as that. For a start, Nathan would have considerable scarring to his face, the hospital had already told him that. His body would be weak and emaciated, to say nothing about the weakness in his voice; he was hearing that for himself. Dynamism was what was needed. Not a skeleton that could barely talk, let alone walk!

The whole damn subterfuge was in severe danger of blowing up in all their faces. Nathan himself would sound the death knell if he re-entered the fray now. Ludlow felt that he must do his level best

Nineteen

to persuade Nathan to stay away from the limelight for just a little longer.

But Nathan was not in a staying away frame of mind. Between a rock and a hard place, Ludlow would have to tell Nathan of his brother's success if he was ever going to persuade him to stay away. He started with the easy option, saying that in his opinion Nathan's weakened appearance would be bound to attract many embarrassing questions.

'Could you not see your way to staying away, at least till inauguration in January, Nathan? This would have a twofold benefit, to allow you to recover properly, and to give the party a chance to stabilize. After all, Julius has been doing so well!' As soon as he said it, Ludlow could have cut his tongue out. He realized he'd blown it.

Nathan's voice hardened. Ludlow could imagine him stiffening up in his hospital bed. 'Is he indeed! What the hell does he know about politics, or anything else for that matter, except how to get into trouble? The sooner I get back there the better. Where are your loyalties, Newt?'

Desperately, Ludlow searched for inspiration, anything. But the well was dry. If things went badly wrong, as they were threatening to do, he would be the one to be blamed.

Nathan's reedy tones sounded harshly down the phone, 'Newt, for Christ's sake! I'm tired of this call. I find your attitude not only baffling, but also downright disloyal. Now do as I ask!'

Down went the phone.

The next day Nathan called him again, this time to say he was dressed and ready to come to Natchez within the next twenty-four hours. His suite was to be ready for him and his schedule of meetings and venues for canvassing to be in a folder ready for him to read. His brother was to be paid off and not only out of his life, but out of Mississippi forever.

'After all, Newt, he's still on parole from prison. He must return to Alabama before someone finds out. Understood?'

Again, Ludlow's mind went into free fall. He had deliberately delayed saying anything to Julius, hoping against hope that Nathan would have a change of heart or, God forgive him, a relapse. But none of this happened. Instead, Nathan had decreed, and his orders must be carried out.

Ludlow knew what Julius's reaction would be. He wasn't wrong.
'Tell him ta go fuck himself. What does he think ah am? Ah haven't built up all these points, gone ta all this trouble, ta make way fer mah straw balled brother! No siree!'

Ludlow pleaded with him, saying he would get him all the money owing to him by the morning. Every bit of it, all cash in hand.

But it was to no avail. Julius had no intention of stepping aside.

Chapter Twenty

As soon as he could, Ludlow put through a scrambled telephone call to the FBI in Natchez. His negotiations to date had been with agent Milt Andersen, who had been surprisingly helpful.

Ludlow opened up about his present dilemma. What was the procedure? What could be done to get Julius to break his parole? Within an hour, after a series of high-level phone calls, Andersen came back to Ludlow. It was agreed that the FBI would lift Julius from the hotel at a pre-arranged time, and spirit him back to prison in Alabama.

Ludlow was left with the extremely distasteful task of forcing Julius to break his parole, which must be done in front of a witness. He decided the best way to achieve this was to force Julius to pick a fight with him, to get him to use his fists. Ludlow would have to say something so personal, so hurtful, that Julius would be bound to respond. This fracas would take place during the course of a normal business meeting.

That evening, with a very heavy heart, Ludlow baited the trap. He despised himself for what he was being forced to do. He set up a meeting with Julius and Margaret Merrylee in Julius's room. A tape recorder was on the table in front of them. There was nothing unusual about that, it was generally there to record business decisions. But it was now required for back up in case something went wrong.

Ludlow was very nervous. He found it more difficult than he'd envisaged to draw Julius into a hostile argument because, far from feeling hostile towards him, he was feeling ashamed. But it had to be done now, with no holds barred. Time was not on their side.

Ludlow knew he couldn't fault Julius for his performance. It was better by far than he'd ever dared hope. He decided to resort to the one painful item, Nathan's return to the scene. Julius must be feeling very raw and threatened about that. If Ludlow rubbed his nose in that it might do the trick. He began the wind-up process.

'You'll have to go, Julius. I'm really very sorry. If it were my decision we would continue with you. Please believe me. It's out of my hands. You do realize that?' Ludlow's haunted eyes said what he genuinely felt.

Julius's response, predictably, was to dig his heels in. 'Ovah mah dead body, Ludlow. Yah know that!'

'Very well, you offer me no alternative.'

Ludlow stood up, walked around the table to where Julius was sitting, leaned down and threw an envelope on the table in front of him. In a surprisingly faltering voice, he said, 'I hereby terminate your contract with the Third Party as from now.'

He pointed to the envelope.

Julius stood up, sweeping the envelope to the floor. His face was crimson with rage. His eyes were burning coals. 'Oh no, y'er not gonna do this ta me!'

He threw a punch at Ludlow. The force of it knocked the burly man to the ground. Margaret Merrylee screamed. This was the signal for the two FBI agents waiting outside to burst through the door and arrest Julius. One of them explained that by his action he had effectively breached the peace and consequently violated the terms of his parole.

By now Julius was foaming at the mouth. He fought like a cornered tiger. At one stage all three were on the floor with Ludlow trying to separate them. Finally, Julius was overpowered and handcuffed.

Julius's final words were fired at Ludlow as he was being taken away.

'Yah set me up, yah rotten treacherous bastard! Y'er dead. Y'er lousy party's dead, and most of all my fuckin' brother's history. Yeh'd better believe it!'

Twenty

Not feeling good about what he'd been forced to do, Ludlow began to have a bad feeling about the whole business. He tried to shake off the feeling of foreboding that had descended on him. Julius's parting words had not helped – not helped at all.

The coast was now officially clear to allow for Nathan's return. But instead of being able to rejoice at his miraculous recovery, the team was dreading the very sight of him. All the spark and enthusiasm had gone out of them. Each felt as if an evil spell had been put on them.

Nathan was in Natchez and Julius was back in prison, all within a few hours. Not for the first time, Ludlow had to pinch himself to ensure he was not dreaming. They had been within an ace of success with Julius – but now?

As he'd expected, Ludlow got a shock when he saw Nathan. He looked a shadow of his former self, pale and with obvious fresh scarring on his face. Despite Nathan's impatience to get on with the job, Ludlow managed to persuade him to delay exposure to the media for one more day. Apart from anything else, the team needed a little time to adjust to his presence.

Using this valuable time, the team composed a press release and fed it to the media. It was to the effect that Nathan had been involved in a minor accident, but had also been suffering from a severe viral infection that had left him drained. This ruse appeared to be successful. There was a marked absence of media questions on the changed state of Senator Beauregarde.

Weak and emaciated though he was, it soon became clear that Nathan had lost none of his old determination. He told them he was fully committed to make up for lost time, to see matters through to a successful conclusion. The next afternoon he held a briefing with the team. Julius's part in the affair was not mentioned. Between them they worked through the schedule Ludlow had prepared, a schedule for canvassing towns and key centers in the time left before elections.

As the days wore on, greatly to Ludlow's relief, little was said from any quarter about Nathan's changed appearance. Perhaps folk genuinely didn't notice. Or, if they did, they were obviously not in the business of making an issue out of it. His spirits began to pick up. Maybe things would be all right after all.

Within a week of his return, Nathan was well and truly back in the driver's seat. He was thinner, and his voice was weaker, but he still had an interesting message to sell. Had they really got away with all the terrible things they had been forced to do during the past few weeks? As time went on without any major disruption, and none of the near impossible explanations that he might have had to make, Newt Ludlow began to breathe more easily.

October was almost out, and the Third Party had already made considerable inroads into people's thinking. With the primaries over, there was a promise of many votes, also offers of money for the party's depleted coffers, coming in daily. Nathan had an open line to his offices in both Washington and New York. In each place there was a fund of goodwill, healthy respect and interest in the party.

By now, Ludlow had climbed out of his slough of despond. He had shaken off the cloak of doom that clung to him for many days after Julius's departure. Nathan had been back in harness for six weeks, and so far as he could judge, they had managed to pull off the biggest con trick of all time, without any damage to the party.

In the absence of public information regarding Julius's existence in the first place, it appeared the public had let any change they imagined they observed go. Ludlow consoled himself with the thought that it was the policies of the Third Party voters were interested in, not what might or might not have gone on behind the scenes. It was only enemies who would be tuned in to seek trouble, and so far they had not emerged from the undergrowth.

Election Day arrived. For the Third Party, the hub of the action was centered around their electoral offices in Natchez. The morning dawned with a heavy mist hanging over the city. But the sun's rays soon dispersed it, turning it into a beautiful day.

Twenty

By now the exhausted team had shot their bolt. There was nothing more they could do. It was very much a case of hope and pray. The building and whole surrounding area was awash with color. Loudspeakers were everywhere, encouraging the undecided to vote for Beauregarde. Flags, bunting, bands and cheerleaders were spread thick as far as the eye could see, all the razzmatazz associated with American Election Day. Election fever had gripped the city. Folk were pouring out of their homes in droves, activated at last to vote for their chosen candidate. Nathan's PR network had been working overtime all day, getting in last minute television time with either members of the team, or sympathetic voters.

Nathan was at his best. He had done a wonderful job of throwing off the effects of his accident. Now he was lean and mean, confident and constantly shaking hands. Late in the afternoon, he mounted the platform to make his final speech.

He had been speaking for a few minutes when his flow was interrupted by a disturbance at the main door of the building. People were shouting, jostling, moving back, making way for someone! A figure broke through the crowd and headed straight for the platform.

Ludlow, standing beside Nathan, shouted, 'My God! It's Julius. He must have broken out of prison!'

'Watch out, he's got a gun!' someone shouted.

A maniac, foam spewing from his mouth, Julius forged forward, revolver pointed directly at Nathan. Realizing what was about to happen, the police and FBI closed in on him. Several tried to disarm him. But Julius was a man with a mission.

Everything appeared to go into slow motion.

'You bastard, you goddamn bastard! I warned you I'd make you pay!' Julius shouted up at the platform.

Nathan, unwilling to duck in front of so many supporters, opened his mouth to protest. Nothing came out.

'Hit the deck, hit the deck!' an FBI agent shouted.

Too late...

Julius fired one shot straight through Nathan's heart, killing him instantly. Senator Beauregarde pitched forward off the platform onto the floor beneath. Pandemonium broke out, men yelling, women and children screaming.

Another shot. This time an FBI agent had fired at Julius. He too keeled over onto the floor beside his brother. Dead. The Third Party's dream was over.

Leaderless at a very vital time, and in such dreadful circumstances, all the remaining spirit had finally drained from Ludlow and the other prime movers in the party. Ironically, even though many all over the country cast their votes that day in the party's favor, it was now as effectively dead as its leader.

In terminal decline from the moment Nathan Beauregarde was gunned down by his brother, it faltered, and before Inauguration Day in January of the following year, it had finally ceased to exist.

And, as the entire world knows, Ronald Reagan, the Republican Party's nominated candidate, became the fortieth President of the United States of America.